A

CHARMING

Corpse

Magical Cures Mystery Series
Book Eleven

Acknowledgements

Thank you to all the June Heal readers! She's such an amazing character and I'm beyond thrilled that after all of these years, eleven books later, everyone is still loving her and all the gang in Whispering Falls!

Big thanks to Sheryl Hagan-Booth for her expert editing skills and Jessica Fischer for the cover art and design. I'm truly blessed to have an amazing team on this journey.

Xoxoxo~
T.

List of June Heal's charms and what they mean.

Turtle Charm: Be sure and steady on your journey.

Silver owl: Wisdom, mysticism, and secrets.

Purple stone in mesh: Clarity and awareness.

Angel Wing: Guidance from above and protection.

Dove sitting on a gold circle: Devotions and hopefulness.

Third eye charm: Peer past illusions.

Small potion bottle: Harm to none.

Brass bell: Beware of comings and goings.

Spiral silver charm: Be aware of your surroundings.

Leaf charm: Seasonal and transitional changes.

Hand of the Fatima: Wards off evil spirits.

Chapter One

Oh, what a difference a year makes. There was something special about the excitement of the warm weather and the hustle and bustle of the village with all the new shops open for the first time since the winter had woken up. Or maybe it was the smell of the cinnamon and sugar coming out of Wicked Good Bakery every time someone opened the door.

There was no denying that Raven Mortimer not only had a talent for Aleruomancy, which was the spiritual gift of being able to ask and receive for messages in dough, but for giving everyone who walked into her bakery a satisfied sweet tooth. Wicked Good Bakery was a great cover up for Raven's gift and still be able to live amongst the mortals.

That's the way it is with all the shops in Whispering Falls, Kentucky.

I needed to grab some sweet treats for a dinner party I was hosting tonight, but the long line of customers Raven had had me detour to The Gathering Grove Tea Shoppe. There was nothing like a great cup of coffee to jumpstart my day.

Mr. Prince Charming, my fairy-god cat, must've thought the same thing because he stiffened his tail and pointed it towards the tea shop before he darted in that direction.

"Good morning, sisters." I pinched a smile when I saw the Karima sisters huddled together at one of the café tables in front of the Gathering Grove Tea Shoppe. It was a little early for the sisters to be out, I thought as I shuffled my feet a little faster hoping to squeak by them.

No such luck. The two grey-haired sisters jumped up from their seats. Their matching red housedresses swooshed up and then down.

"June Heal," Constance Karima waddled over to me before I could scurry into the tea shop. "Just the person we wanted to see."

"Yes. Just the person," Patience repeated with a sinister giggle. "Yes. Just the person," she repeated again like she always did.

It was their thing. Constance made the first words of conversation and Patience repeated her. Or maybe it was just Patience's way of being seen outside as the more outgoing of the twins, not to mention, Patience was shorter than the two, though not leaner.

"Good to see you too." I nodded and tucked a strand of hair behind my ear. Mr. Prince Charming rubbed his body in and out between my ankles in a figure 8, assuring me everything was fine.

"We smell death." Constance's chin lifted up and she sniffed the air.

That got my attention. The Karima sisters had the spiritual gift of Ghost Whispering but it didn't end there. They were able to smell the ghost before the ghost knew it was going to be a ghost. I gulped and looked down at Mr. Prince Charming for more assurance than just the figure 8. He had nothing to give me. He sat down and drew his paw up to his mouth, giving it a good couple of licks.

I was going to have to rely on my gift of intuition to test the air. I gulped again, closed my eyes, drew my hands together in a prayer pose, took a deep breath then began turning side-to-side getting air from all directions. The fresh air floated down and seeped into every corner of my body as I grounded into my inner self. A smile crossed my face as the joy of happiness swirled around me.

"Mmmhmmm, death," Patience whispered, bringing me out of my trance. Her green eyes snapped at me before she drew them down towards the ground, bending down to take a whiff of Mr. Prince Charming.

Mewl, Mr. Prince Charming, my fairy-god cat, batted at Patience, quickly making her pop back up to standing.

"Oh, sisters." I put one hand on each of their backs and took a few steps towards the counter. I'd decided to go with my intuition. "That's not death. That's life. Life of the winter falling away and Mother Nature waking the world up to a new season."

"That's life after death. That's what it is." Constance nodded and grabbed Patience by the arm. "Let's go, sister. June Heal isn't helping us. As it appears she's not helping the community."

Constance reached over and picked up a flyer off the counter, shoving it in my chest before the two of them waddled off and out of the tea shop. I quickly glanced at the piece of paper.

"Want to feel better? Are you having trouble sleeping? Trying to lose that extra weight but no matter what you do, you just can't?" I read. "Try Life Choice Homeopathic today. Come by Crazy Craft Chicks from three p.m. to six p.m. Monday." I looked up and got lost in thought. "Today is Monday," I whispered.

My gut went into a spiral downslide and then into an upswing, causing me to get a little dizzy. I might not have a sense death was knocking on Whispering Falls, but I did wonder if this new homeopathic service was what had made my business slow down.

"Making the sisters mad?" Gerald Reguila twirled the edge of his mustache with his thumb and finger with a curious look in his eye.

"Oh, my." I giggled. "Who doesn't make the sisters mad?"

"You are a very wise one." Gerald winked and tapped his top hat. "Your usual?"

"I'd like an extra shot of espresso." I gripped the paper and waded it up in my fist. "Something tells me I'm going to need it."

While I waited for Gerald to make my coffee, I walked over to the window and looked across the street at Crazy Crafty Chick. It was a fairly new shop and owned by Leah LeRoy.

From what I knew about Leah, she was from Alabama and a clairsentience, which meant she was able to pick up sensations and relate messages from sensations.

"Here you go." Gerald handed me a mug of coffee. "You can sit here and enjoy." He pointed to the table next to us.

"I'm sorry. I should've said to-go," I said, knowing exactly what Gerald was up to.

"I should've asked." He gave a sly smile and turned around, the tails on his tuxedo jacket swirled around and flapped with each of his strong strides to the back of the shop.

Meow, Mr. Prince Charming sat down next to me. Just like me, he knew that Gerald was trying to pull a slick one on me, which wasn't unlike him. Gerald was a tealeaf reader and he took every opportunity to offer a complementary reading to anyone who came into the shop.

Though it was Rule Number One in our spiritual by-laws of Whispering Falls, no other spiritual can read another spiritualist without their permission. Gerald always tried to get around that law by having the spiritualist drink from a teacup, paper cup, mug or any other object he served drinks in just so he could happen to get a look at the bottom residue. No doubt in my mind was he trying to see just exactly what was going on between me and the Karima sisters.

"You need to remind me when it's 3 p.m." I told Mr. Prince Charming. "We've got a homeopathic party to go to."

Rowl, Rowl. Mr. Prince Charming stood up on his hind legs and batted at my charm bracelet dangling. It was the signal he gave me to trust in what he's given me so far.

"You know exactly what I need." I bent down to pat him just as someone opened the door of the shoppe and he darted out the open door.

"Looks like someone is in a hurry." Gerald held the cup out and glanced over my shoulder, out the window at Mr. Prince Charming darting across the street.

"I guess something caught his fancy." I took the cup. "Give my best to Petunia and Orin," I said about his wife and baby as a way of cutting off the small talk and getting back to my shop.

I had about ten minutes to walk down there and open up for the day. Not that I expected a line like Raven and Gerald had with their shops, because frankly, business had been slow.

It was something I'd chalked up to the cold weather that'd blanketed our little dug out hollow in the state that kept mortals or tourist coming through, but now I wasn't so sure.

I took a sip of my coffee and glanced at the rumpled-up piece of paper in my hand.

I definitely wasn't so sure now.

Chapter Two

The sudden burst of wind caught the sign that dangled in front of my shop and swung it back and forth making a creaking sound. I reached up, stopping the sign from swinging.

"A Charming Cure, formerly A Dose Of Darla," I said out loud and wiped my hand across it.

Darla Heal was my mother and this had been her shop. I didn't remember much of that time since I was just a child. She was a mortal that'd married my father, the spiritualist. He was a police officer killed in the line of duty.

Oh, how times had changed. I smiled to myself wondering what it'd been like if the by-laws then had allowed my mother and me to live in Whispering Falls after my father's death even though it stated that no mortals shall live within the limits of the spiritual community.

After discovering my true identity as a spiritualist at the age of eighteen and after Darla had died, I moved to Whispering Falls. It was a no-brainer that since I was born with my father's DNA that I'd reopen her shop and run it the way she intended.

The small cottage house, I'd left the same. The ornamental gate opened up onto a walkway that lead underneath the most beautiful pergola with beautiful white and purple Wisteria vines. The front of the shop had a window framing each side of the door that was perfect for the sunshine that would be dripping through them in a couple of hours.

I trotted up the steps and looked both ways before I used the old skeleton key to open the

door. Once inside, my heart leapt up into my throat and made my lips turn upward into the biggest smile as it always did when I opened up for the day.

As I walked through the shop, I ran my hands along the tops of the items, saying a small blessing to each one. The presentation was very important to Darla and I'd taken great pride in keeping with the way she did business.

The shop had two rooms.

The front room, where all the hard work of my hard was on display, was filled with all sorts of glass bottles of different shapes and sizes. A Charming Cure might sell homeopathic cures, but the true magic was in the bottle, made specific for each person who walked through my shop doors.

The customer might think they were coming in for a heartburn medication, when in reality they're suffering from a broken heart. With my spiritual gift, I was able to concoct a true healing remedy and this. . .this. . .I thought as I gripped the flyer that I was still holding, had phony written all over it. At least that's what my intuition told me.

The bell over the door dinged a few times as Chandra Shango walked in.

"Good morning," Chandra Shango trilled, giving her cape a good tug around her neck, letting it fall around her back. Mr. Prince Charming darted in before she shut the door.

"Be careful," I quickly ran across the room to catch the decorative lamp on the table that he'd ran under, having caught the red table cloth with his paws, causing it to shift.

The lamps were scattered throughout the shop on small tables with a different ornamental lampshade on each one. Mr. Prince Charming had a habit of running under them to hide and he never watched out for what he was doing. He was good at knocking over my potion bottles and the lamps.

An easy solution would be to take the lamps off all the tables, but it felt homey and warmed the place. If I was to spend countless hours a week in here, I certainly wanted it to feel like home and not a job.

"How are you this morning?" I asked Chandra and headed back to the counter to get everything ready for opening.

"Booked, booked, and booked." She adjusted the black turban on top of her head and drummed her fingers together while looking around.

I smiled as the perfectly painted green nails flashed with small flowers on each of them. She truly was an artist that, with the help of her spiritual gift, had flourished..

"I'm all out of hand cream and I've got several pedicures to do today." She exclaimed.

"You mean foot cream?" I asked, putting the coffee down on the counter and the waded-up flyer. I took my purse that was strapped across my body, and hung it on the back of the chair before disappearing behind the partition that separated the counter into two parts.

"No. Manicures. I know what I mean." She corrected me and I didn't bother asking why. She knew what she needed for A Cleansing Spirit Spa, the shop next to mine where Chandra was a palm reader.

"Oh, okay. I've got some general itchy palm, which means money, and some. . ." I flipped on my cauldron and popped my head from around the partition. "What are you doing?" I asked Chandra when I realized that she'd just bought a whole bunch of cream that should have lasted her the rest of the month.

"Actually." She lowered her eyes. "I wanted to know how you were doing."

"Then why didn't you ask as soon as you came in?" I questioned my longtime friend. "Since when did we dance around each other?" I asked and walked around the counter.

"Since I heard that your feelings could be hurt from the flyer you picked up at the tea shop," her voice trailed off.

"Well." I reached over to the counter and held up my cup of coffee. "I know Gerald didn't have the opportunity to read my coffee grounds, and I haven't heard the paper yet, so the Karimas?" I eyed her. She turned away. "But I have to wonder why one of my dearest friends didn't tell me about this new homeopathic option in Whispering Fall?"

"Oh, June. You know I adore you and Darla. I've loved you since the first day you were born, but this." She swept across the floor and jabbed the paper with her long fingernail. "This is not of the spiritual realm. This is the mortals trying to capture exactly what you have here." She drew her arms in front of her as though she were conducting an orchestra.

"I'm going to see for myself." I tapped my finger on my watchless wrist. "3 p.m. right, Mr. Prince Charming?" My chin lifted in the air to carry my voice.

The tip of Mr. Prince Charming's tail was barely visible from underneath the long, flowing tablecloth. It swept back and forth a couple of times in a slow motion.

"You think that's a good idea?" Chandra asked.

I picked up the chalkboard eraser and walked over to the wall where the chalkboard hung and erased yesterday's special so I could write today's..

"I'd like to check out my competition, yes. It's a fine idea." I wrote, Put your spring back into your step with a boost of energy~ Kali Phos.

"If you insist." She gnawed on the edge of her lip as her brows drew together. "Do you insist?" She asked.

"I insist. Now, do you really need hand cream?" I knew she didn't. My intuition told me so, but I wanted to make sure. It seemed my intuition had appeared to be off since I really couldn't put a finger as to why my business had slowed down.

"Well." She swooped around the shop, fingering all the tiered displays with of my remedies on them.

While she took her time trying to decide whether it was right for her to purchase something from me, or my competition, I picked up the feather duster from behind the counter and shook it in the air. *Cough, cough.* I fanned the dust to make way for more to collect on the duster. Walking from display to display, I swiped them each so when the beautiful sun that Mother Nature had promised for today would send in her rays of amazing sunshine to bestow upon the bottles, they would gleam.

"I think I'm good." She wiggled her fingers. "Ta-ta."

"Mmmhmmmm," I hummed through my nose and headed to the back room.

The back room walls were originally lined with every ingredient that I had ever dreamed of, but I moved them to the shelves behind the counter so I could make my potions while watching the shop at the same time.

The back had become sort of a break room for extra things like the dried herbs that hung from a clothesline around the room. There were burners, test tubes, melting pots, strainers, muslin cloths, cauldrons and much more. There was a desk, mini-refrigerator, and a couch that was a good place to rest if I ever needed to. And some days I needed to.

The sound of the bell over the front door dinged again, putting a little hope in my gut that today was going to be a good sales day.

"Good morning," I said and pushed through the door between the storage room and the shop. "Raven."

My heart sank.

"That." She circled her finger in front of my face. "Isn't happy I'm here." She drew her hand to her chest. "I'm hurt."

"No. It's not you."

"It's not you, it's me?" She winked mocking the break up moniker.

"Not that I'm not happy to see you, my dear friend." I hugged her and then took the pink bag she gave me with the Wicked Good logo on the front. "It's just that business has been a little down and when I heard the bell. . ." My head teetered side-to-side in a you know kinda way.

"I heard about the…" Her eyes drew over my shoulder and she looked at the brochure before she finished her sentence. "The homeopathic thingy."

"You can say it." I shrugged. "My competition."

That's the thing. There'd been no competition between the businesses in Whispering Falls because all of the shop owners had a special spiritual gift. None of us were alike, then a year or so ago, the Order Of Elders decided that we could move from village to village and open up space for mortal neighborhoods.

"It does seem to be a first for all of us." Her black eyes impaled me. "And there's no way someone could ever be better than you."

"You are too kind, but Darla would say that there's room enough for everyone." I turned my head towards the right wall and looked at the framed photo of my parents. It was the only photo I had of them. "When I was a little girl, Darla, you know she didn't let me call her mom." I laughed at the memory. "Anyways, she and I would pack up her little car and we'd go to the flea market for the day. Whenever I'd see people there selling soaps and other items that could be considered in Darla's wheelhouse, I'd get mad. That's when she'd spout out all of her worldly wisdom."

"That's why you are so nice and kind, June Heal. And why I decided to bake you some June's Gems this morning," she said matter-of-factly as her chin drew a hard line up and then down.

"I couldn't think of anything I'd rather eat for breakfast." I opened the bag and took one out, taking a big bite.

"It's worse than I thought." Raven's voice died away.

"What are you talking about?" I muffled with a full mouth of delicious chocolaty treat that Raven had created with my name since I was addicted to Ding Dongs. I drew my hand back and looked at the half-eaten June's Gem. "Oh, no."

The sudden urge to cry flooded my throat and left a big knot there. I gulped and gulped again, only harder.

"You saw something in the dough, didn't you?" I questioned what her spiritual gift had told her.

Slowly, she lifted her head and down, her jaw set tight.

"I'm not sure what it's all about, but I got a reading that you needed some stress relief and in our history, I knew the only thing you liked when you were stressed were Ding Dongs." She sucked in a deep sigh. "Want to talk?"

"Like I said, business has been down, but I attributed it to winter, but now my gut tells me that my customers have found a new homeopathic shop." I rolled my eyes. "I can't even say it's a shop." I stuffed the rest of the June's Gem in my mouth.

"From what I understand, it's more like one of those mortal parties where people host them at their houses." She picked up a blue bottle with gold flecks off of one of the display tables. She lifted the cork lid and took a smell. "Nothing like what you have here." She carefully put the bottle back on the table.

"It's a mortal doing the cures?" I asked. She nodded. "She's a modern day Darla." I smiled remembering how Darla would work for hours in her little work shed in the back yard of our Locust Grove house.

She'd spend so much time out there trying to read the Magical Cures Book that she set more stuff on fire than actually making cures. Then again, she wasn't a spiritualist, so the Magical Cures Book did her no good.

"Maybe it's a fad." The heels of my shoes clicked on my way over to the door to turn the sign to open. "I've got to pay the bills somehow. You didn't see anything else in the dough?"

"I just saw potion bottles and felt sadness. Naturally, I thought of you." She walked over to the door and stopped next to me. "If you need a friend, I'm always here."

"Nah," I waved her off and put on a smile. "I'm fine."

I'm always fine, I thought and shut the door after her.

Chapter Three

The afternoon dragged on. There were a few people who I couldn't even call customers. They were either looking for directions to a different shop or had gotten lost on their way to another town.

Meow.

Mr. Prince Charming jumped up on the counter and dragged his tail underneath my nose. The little tickle gave me a jolt to my afternoon slumber.

Meow, meow. He continued to badger me.

"What's going on with you?" I asked and popped up. "It's three o'clock."

I glanced around my empty shop and realized if there weren't any customers by now, there probably wouldn't be in the next couple of hours. Mr. Prince Charming knew exactly what I was thinking. He jumped off the counter and scurried over to the door. I grabbed my bag and threw it over my shoulder. I took out another June's Gem from the Wicked Good pouch before shoving it into my bag.

"I better eat this just in case I feel a little stress." I glanced at Mr. Prince Charming and took a big bite, letting the gooeyness settle in my soul. Before I knew it, the entire thing was gone. I flipped my cauldron off and the lights, along with the sign to CLOSED, locking the door behind me.

"Let's get out of here and see exactly what this stuff is all about," I told Mr. Prince Charming.

He darted way ahead of me. His tail swayed up in the air, stopping briefly for people on the street to try to pat him before he teased them by running away as their hand came down to give him a pat.

Crazy Crafty Chick was a fairly new shop I'd only been in a handful of times. Mr. Prince Charming found the baskets of yarn on the front porch of the blue-colored cottage shop very comfortable for his late afternoon naps. Leah, the owner, acted as though it didn't bother her, but I thought it to be rude.

She stood at the white fence that was around the shop, letting in customers through the wrought-iron gate as they came in one by one. While I stood waiting in line, I ran my hand over the ornamental gate that had images of thread, needles, glass beads and pottery tools. Every shop had an ornamental gate that represented what their shop was about.

"June, I'm. . ." Leah's lips curled in, her eyes narrowed. She appeared to be fighting to find words.

"Surprised to see me?" I asked.

Her silence spoke volumes.

"Why? I don't just shop for sweet treats at Wicked Good. I get some from The Gathering Grove and sometimes I buy Mr. Prince Charming's cat food at the Piggly Wiggly in Locust Grove, not just Glorybee," I said, hoping to ease her tension.

"You know how it is. I'm new and when Gabby asked me if she could host her line of products here, I didn't realize she'd be posting flyers all over Whispering Falls." Leah pushed back her long brown hair over her shoulder and offered a sympathetic smile.

"Really," I assured her in my best lie. "I'm here as a customer."

"Welcome," she said in her sweet southern voice, pushing the gate open for me to walk down the little front walk and up the steps to her shop's cute front porch.

Gabby Summerfield, or who I assumed was Gabby that Leah had mentioned outside, was greeting everyone at the door with a small knitted bag. There was a note attached to it.

"Hi, there. I'm Gabby Summerfied. I'm the local representative for Lifestyle. I'm so glad you came. Where or who did you hear about the event from?" Her head tilted to the side. She had black hair that was cut short up the back and a little longer on the sides. She had long bangs on the left side and thick eyebrows.

"I was at The Gathering Grove this morning and saw your flyer on the counter." I tapped into my gut intuition and got nothing.

"Here is a little gift for coming." She handed me the pouch. "Leah spent a week teaching me how to make these little pouches. I'm so glad that's over because I'm not crafty at all." She giggled and moved on to the next person.

Once inside, I looked around the craft shop. I'd done a couple of ceramic things over the holidays with a girls' night out deal, but never really looked around. There was a deep-set envy in my soul as I noticed all the customers in the shop. It wasn't long ago that I remembered A Charming Cure was hopping like this.

I hurried over to the wall of yarn so no one would see me upset. There were spools and rows of yarn that were hanging like rolls of paper towels. It was an interesting display that worked well for yarn. Leah had them arranged by color. As I ran my hand along the tops of them, I never realized there were different textures of yarn.

"Girls," I heard a familiar voice behind me. "Gerald told me that June. . ."

I turned around and my eyes met Petunia Shurbwood's eyes.

"June," her voice rose an octave. "I was just saying that Gerald saw you this morning."

"You were. I heard." I tapped my ear knowing that she was going to say more than just that until she saw me.

She was standing amongst people I called my friends. Amethyst Plum, Bella Vanlow, Isadora Solstice, and Ophelia Biblio. They all appeared to be shocked to see me as they all either looked down at their feet or in other directions.

"What's going on here? I suddenly feel like an outsider." I tried to make eye contact with them.

"Oh, June," Petunia whined. "We love you."

"Yes. We all love you." Ophelia reached out to touch my arm.

"And we would never want to hurt our friend's feelings." Bella pinched a smile. Her eyes were soft.

"I told them there was no good in coming from this. As the oldest member of our village, I discouraged this. But no." Isadora, Izzy for short, wagged her long finger in the air. She mocked, "We'll just go to see what Lifestyle is all about."

"I agreed with Izzy. I told them that you were the real deal and this stuff definitely couldn't be. Look at the price." Amethyst Plum, owner of Fullmoon Tree Resort, and one of my biggest clients for a lavender sleep spray she pumped into her guests' bedrooms at night so they got a great night's sleep and would be sure to return, held a bottle of sleep spray up in my face. "Five dollars. Come on, it can't be real. Your stuff is twice this price."

There was a slight warm feeling against my side where my bag rested. It was a sure sign that my crystal ball, Madame Torres, had woken for the day and was ready to give me any insight on what was going on in the spiritual world.

"Then why is everyone here?" I asked and turned around to notice every shop owner in Whispering Falls had walked into the Crazy Crafty Chick shop "And, I had no clue about it until today?" I asked.

"Wait." I hit my intuition and I knew I was right on the mark. Especially when I notice Faith Mortimer, the editor-in-chief of the spiritual newspaper taking camera shots of all the products. "Did this announcement go into the Whispering Falls Gazette and Faith Mortimer conveniently leave me out of it?"

"Ummm. . .well. . ." Petunia's eyes dipped. "I told Gerald to take those flyers off his counter," she spat like it was Gerald's fault I found out.

"Listen, I was going to find out one way or another. I really appreciate your friendship and I do understand why you've been trying so hard to keep it from me, but I'm not sure why." I made a point to look at them. "She isn't a spiritualist and I'm sure she's just passing through like most of those home parties the mortals do. Now that it's getting warmer, I'm sure business will pick up and Whispering Falls will once again be thriving." I put my hand on my bag as the warming sensation got hot. "If you'll excuse me. I'm going to go look around."

My back was met with hushed whispers as I walked by people I knew. There was no way of getting around the gossip that was just plain untrue. I wasn't mad. What I was feeling was hurt that my friends didn't come to me and tell me about this new line of products that could potentially hurt my business. If I was being totally honest, I'm sure it's what hurt my business. I've weathered many storms before, One of the biggest was learning that after eighteen years I was, as the mortals would refer to me, a witch,. Now, that was a storm that took some life-altering changes. *This shall pass*, as Darla would say.

"I can't believe you," I heard someone whisper as I turned into another room so I could see exactly what Madame Torres was wanting so urgent from my bag. "You are a crook and I'm not going to let you get away with it. So you're going to have to kill me to keep my mouth shut."

There was a loud slam, a crash, and when I turned the corner, Gabby Summerfield's face was flush red with anger as she stood at the back door of the shop. Alone.

"Gabby," I reached out and it brought her out of the rage.

Her face softened and her lips curled up in a smile.

"Hi," she trilled as if nothing happened.

"Are you okay?" I asked and peeked out the door. There was no one or nothing there.

"I'm fine." Her hands brushed down her shirt. "Why do you ask?" Her shoulders drew back, making her stand up straighter.

"I thought I heard you yelling at someone and the door slam." I gestured to the door.

"Oh, gosh." She laughed. "I was trying to carry too much and dropped a bottle. I was fussing at myself." She crunched up her nose and pulled her shoulders to her ears. She bent down and picked up the broken glass and used a napkin to sop up the liquid.

"I'll see you in the other room." She threw the wet napkin into the garbage can.

"I'll be right there," I said, knowing she'd just lied to me. But why would she care? "I need to make a phone call."

That satisfied her because she threw the last bits of broken glass in the garbage can and went back into the front of the shop, leaving me there to pull out Madame Torres.

"Hello, June Heal." Madame Torres's green eyes stood out around her red medusa hair that flowed inside the glass globe. The water around her illuminated with yellow, red, orange, and purple lines. "There is danger lurking here."

Her eyes were gaunt and darted back and forth like she was looking outside of the ball's edges. "There's no good reason for you to be here," she spoke, her lips were rosy red, and her skin was pale. "You should leave. Immediately!" Her voice was demanding and shrill as the water swirled orange, pink and a violent shade of red before she went dark.

"Madame Torres." I shook her. "You can't just leave it like this." I shook her harder.

Mewl. Mr. Prince Charming trotted into the back room and dropped something at my feet.

My heart sank. The room began to spin as my eyes focused on what he'd laid at my feet. My mouth dried. I licked my lips as the aura of colors took over my peripheral vision, leaving me with a tunnel of light on the charm.

"I see our little friend has given you his present." Bella Von Low brought me out of my trance. She bent down, her long blonde hair swept over her shoulder, grazing the floor as she swooped up to stand then outstretched her arm with the charm nestled in the cup of her palm. "Oh, the Eye of the Fatima. Protection and to trust in your intuition."

I focused on her palm, not wanting to take yet another charm from my fairy-god cat. The first time I'd met Mr. Prince Charming was on my tenth birthday. Darla didn't have a lot of money. Though she didn't get me any sort of present, she did get me a cake from the Piggly Wiggly she'd gotten on sale because it read *Happy Retirement Stu.* Apparently, Stu didn't get his cake and Darla didn't even bother scraping Stu's message off.

It was a treat because Darla never let me eat any type of sweets except on my birthday and I attribute my crazy addiction to Ding Dongs to the fact I was deprived.

On that day, a little white stray cat had popped up on the steps of our front porch. He was the brightest of white I'd ever seen. He had on a faded collar with a tiny turtle charm dangling from it. The turtle was missing one of the green emerald stones for an eye, but it was beautiful.

Oscar and I asked around to see if the cat belonged to anyone, even making posters out of the Piggly Wiggly brown grocery bags, but no one claimed him. When he continued to hang around, I decided to keep him. Darla didn't mind as long as she didn't have to buy food for him. I got him a new collar for cheap at the flea market and kept the turtle charm for myself. Oscar had given me his mom's old bracelet and I hung it from there.

Little did I know that Mr. Prince Charming was sent by the village to keep watch over me until I turned eighteen years old so they could see if I was a spiritualist like my father. If I was, then they'd invite me to live in Whispering Falls and by the outcome, you can see that I took them up on their offer.

It wasn't until I moved to Whispering Falls that I felt like I belonged to a community. I was surrounded by people who not only knew my parents, but also understood my weird quirks, which happened to be my witch abilities. I'd also discovered Mr. Prince Charming was my fairy-god cat and the way he communicated lurking danger was to bring me charms that had some sort of symbolic meaning.

"I'm assuming he came to see you today?" I slipped the charm from Bella's palm and took a look at it.

"He came to the shop and went straight to the charm. No hesitation." Bella owned Bella's Baubles, the local jewelry store. It was a perfect cover up for her ability as an astrologer spiritualist.

"He's got to stop stealing charms." I wanted to scold him since it took the feelings off of me and put them on him, but it wasn't working.

"Is that really what you mean? Or do you mean that you don't want to tap into your gift and figure out what this means?" Bella smiled, her cheeks balled and exposed the gap between her two front teeth. Her five foot two inch petite frame might've been small, but she was larger than life and very wise.

"I got a strange message a few minutes ago from Madame Torres." I normally never told anyone when my crazy crystal ball had a reading for me. "She said danger was lurking."

Bella reached up and cupped my hand with the Fatima charm. The warmth of the union, caused me to suck in a deep breath. A sense of calm swept over me. Bella unclasped the charm bracelet off of my wrist.

"You stop by and get this from me later tonight." She always put the charms on my bracelet that Mr. Prince Charming had given me. This would be the twelfth charm and none of them have come with just a warning and not a life-changing event.

"I'm having Eloise and Adeline over for a cookout tonight to celebrate the coming of the spring solstice after the smudging ceremony if you'd like to join us and bring the bracelet." It was the least I could do for all she's done for me.

"I'd be honored." She bowed her head. "I think I'm going to slip out the back door. This isn't for me." She pointed to the shop where Gabby had started giving the information about the products she was selling.

"Traitor," I called after Mr. Prince Charming when he darted out the door with Bella.

I rubbed my naked wrist and said a little spell of protection, "Protect all who dwell here too. Protect this place where we reside. Protect with light that is true."

Chapter Four

"Of course, you want to feel better," Gabby said and looked around the room at all the eager faces. "Are you sad? Do you harbor ill feelings? Are you stressed?"

Her words were met with heads bobbing yes, nudging the people next to them, and few a who even yelled yes.

"Then look no further." Gabby grabbed one of the clear bottles, out of hundreds that were sitting on the table next to her. They all had the same bottle, same form, but different colored labels made them stand apart from the rest.

"Your bottles are prettier," Petunia leaned over and whispered in my ear.

I didn't want to be rude and talk to Petunia while Gabby was giving her presentation on her fake product, so I kept in my rant about how my bottles actually have magic and they pick their owner.

It was true. When someone came in with an ailment, I knew what they really needed and would let them pick out what they thought they needed. Then I'd run my fingers down my bottle collection. That's when the magic truly happened. All of my bottles were ornamental, and glowed with delight when their owner would come into the shop. A few swirls around my cauldron, a little touch of magical herbs, and I'd bottle their very own personal potion to sell to them.

Of course, they had no idea that I was actually curing what they had. They only knew they instantly felt better after using it and continued to be repeat customers. Until….Gabby.

I looked around and saw a few faces from customers who'd traveled far and wide to get their bottles refilled. There was no way I was going to be able to jump up and scream that Gabby's product was a fraud, so I was going to have to wait and see if the customer realized it didn't work and come back to A Charming Cure.

"You!" Gabby pointed at me. "What is hurting you?"

"Me?" I pointed to myself and looked around.

"Yes. You." She smiled and nodded. "What would you like to bring more into your life?"

"Calm." It was the first word that set my intuition in motion. I wanted calm in the community that I feared was on the cusp of a wave that was going to wash over our small village.

"Perfect." She reached over and grabbed a clear bottle with a yellow label. "Come here," she waved me to the front of the room.

There was a hush that came over my friends. Gabby clearly had no idea the spiritual community she was in.

"Why don't you pick someone else?" Izzy encouraged Gabby. "June is already. . ."

"No, I'd love to try it." I brushed Izzy off. "I'll never know until I try."

"I'm not sure this is a good idea," Izzy said in a hushed voice when I made my way to the front of the room.

"I think it's a perfect idea." I smiled and patted her on the back. "This is fun," I assured her.

"For who?" Izzy cocked a brow and pushed back a strand of her curly blonde hair.

"Isn't this the cutest crochet pouch?" She asked. "You can put your roll-on bottle in it and hook it to your purse." She looked around. "I'm not sure where she is, but your very own, Leah and I had a business deal and she's made these. You really need to buy one along with your roll-on oil. Now, you'll need to rub this on your temples, inside of the wrist, and roll it down the back of the neck." Gabby watched as I took the small bottle and did what she said.

"I smell Sage, Lavender, Bergamot, Roman Chamomile, Cedarwood, Ylang Ylang, Geranium, Fennel, Carrot Seed, Palmarosa, and Vitex." I did what she said and handed the bottle back to her. "While these are a wonderful combination, how exactly will they calm my nerves? Does this seep into the skin? Get into my soul?"

"And we need a coffee." Faith Mortimer walked over to me and grabbed me by the elbow, rushing me out the front door.

"Why did you do that?" I asked and lifted my chin to feel the warmth of the sun on my face.

"Because you and I both know that she just throws herbs together. Remember how Darla started?" She reminded me that Darla had made a good living doing exactly what Gabby was doing and she wasn't a spiritualist either.

"Then she needs to go to the flea market in Locust Grove," I suggested. "Besides, why did you take me off the subscription list of the paper this morning?"

"She took an ad out in the paper copy and Leah had asked me to put it in the spiritual edition." Faith and I darted across the street. We really couldn't talk with the sidewalks and street full of people.

Faith and I had come a long way with our relationship since we'd met in Intuition School during my brief stint at Hidden Hall, A Spiritual University. She and I didn't see eye-to-eye at first, but we are the greatest of friends now, along with her sister Raven.

I pushed open the large wooden pink door that lead into the charming confectionary. Raven was behind the counter facing the ovens. She had her long black hair knotted down her back in a fishtail braid and pink Wicked Good Bakery apron tied around her neck and waist. She was taking out some sweet treats to cool.

"I didn't want to hurt your feelings and didn't want you to think we were all trying to promote her business, but I have to be fair with the other shop owners. Leah did pay to put it in there." Faith's mouth dipped into a frown.

We stepped into the bakery. Jars of candy lined the lime green walls and made a wonderful array of colors that would make anyone want to purchase the sweets. Raven had placed cake stands on each table in the middle of the shop with most amazing assortment of cupcakes and scones, not to mention a few June's Gems. She let people come in and pick out what they wanted.

Some might think the treats sitting out in the open would get stale, but they didn't realize there was magic in each one and that little bit of love kept them warm and fresh.

"Next time, let me decide what is good and not good for me. I pay for the paper to be air delivered and I want it every morning." I wasn't going to let her get off that easy.

The Whispering Falls Gazette was delivered through the breeze of the morning wind to all the spiritualists in the village who subscribed to it. It was no different than waking up to a physical newspaper delivered to your mailbox, only it was read in Faith's voice and through the breeze.

It was the best practice not to have any sort of magical or spiritual paper copies as we lived amongst the mortals. It wasn't until the new neighborhood opened up that the paper was printed for their benefit. Mainly it consisted of sales from the shops. Anything we had to discuss was done during the weekly smudging ceremony with the village President and council members.

"I was just taking your order out of the oven." Raven smiled, looking down at her creation. "Lemon Yogurt Cake."

The sound of it made my mouth water. I peeked over the counter at the loaf pans filled with the tan and buttery cakes.

"I've just got to drizzle some deliciousness over the top and put it in a box so you can take it." She took a glass pitcher filled with icing and carefully held it over one of the pans and let the white sugary mix zig-zag down over the cake.

"I want to skip the food and just go straight to the dessert," I said. "Are you sure you didn't see anything in the dough besides the intuition?" I asked about how she'd brought me some June's Gems this morning on a whim.

"I. . .um. . ." She sat the glass pitcher down and looked up at me. "I had an image of the Fatima hand with the eye."

"The exact charm Mr. Prince Charming brought me." I gnawed on the information. "Why didn't you tell me?"

"All the rules we have around here now, you just never know who's listening." She looked up into the open air. Then she busied herself with taking my Lemon Yogurt Cake out of the pan and placing it into one of the Wicked Good Bakery boxes.

She was right. The Order of Elders were always floating around from village to village, making sure we were following the spiritualist rules so the mortals wouldn't find out about us or even the evil spiritualist out there.

"From now on, why don't the two of you leave it up to me to decide what's best for me." My eyes slid down the counter at the June's Gems. "I'll have one of those too."

"Please tell me you have time for a cup of coffee," Raven's eyes light up. "We need some girl time."

"Maybe one cup." I shrugged and followed the black and white checkered floor that led the way to a room filled with Victorian style dining furniture where customers could go and sit down while they enjoyed a dessert and cup of tea or coffee. Raven and Gerald had a consignment system between their two shops. She provided him with desserts he didn't make and in turn he provided her with his specialty teas.

I sat down in one of the velvet chairs that rested in front of a wooden coffee table and looked around. My insides were feeling much better. I let out a long sigh of happiness when Raven and Faith walked in with a tray of coffee mugs and plates of June's Gems.

There truly wasn't anything like having girlfriends. Right now, I was thinking I was going to need them more than ever with the gut feelings of uneasiness inside me.

Chapter Five

Instead of heading back down to A Charming Cure, I
walked back across the street and straight into Crazy Crafty
Chick Shop. I wasn't sure why I was being called to go
back there, but I did. Maybe it was the combination smells
of Roman Chamomile, Cedarwood, Ylang Ylang from the
Lifestyle calm Gabby had me roll all over my temples and
neck, but I'd like to think it was my intuition that told me to
go back.

I'd learned my lesson when I didn't listen to my
intuition one time and never made that mistake again. It
was getting closer to six p.m., which wasn't only quitting
time for the shops in Whispering Falls, but it was also the
ending time for Gabby's party.

"You're back." Gabby's face brightened when she saw
me walk in. "I have to apologize. I didn't know that you
owned A Charming Cure. Darling shop. But I just sell this
out of my house. I'm trying to pay off college debt and get
into a house of my own."

"You don't need to apologize." I suddenly felt awful for having my jealous feelings for her. "There's plenty of customers to go around."

"I'm so glad you said that." Her head tilted back and forth. Her face relaxed and a sense of calm swept over her. "Honestly, I had to beg Leah to have me. We met at another party in Locust Grove. She said that she lived in Whispering Falls and it's been so mysterious here that I continued to badger her until she said yes."

"Here." I had to make peace and why not with one of the extra June's Gems Raven had sent home with me along with my Lemon Yogurt Cake. "These will make you feel better."

She peeked inside of the bag before she reached in. She took a bite.

"Mmmm." A satisfied sigh oozed out of her as well as her inner demons.

While she enjoyed the treat, I soaked in her pain. There was a sense of loss, loneliness and money floating around her aura. This was the time when I'd suggest a cure for the customer; only Gabby wasn't one of my customers. I was hers.

"I think I'll take a bottle of each." I pointed knowing that Oscar was going to kill me for spending all this money when he didn't make a whole lot as sheriff and the shop wasn't bringing in much money lately.

"Really?" she asked with dipped brows.

The shift in her aura turned green as her heart melted away some stress, but not all. It'd take me a few times to be with her or even put a few cures in her own bottles for her to try.

"Have you tried your own homeopathic oils?" I questioned.

I couldn't bring myself to say cures because these were no more than a few herbs and oils thrown together. I wasn't saying that peppermint didn't help calm the nerves, it most certainly did. But that was just the layer to many layers of issues that if not attended too would still be there.

"Yes." She pulled out a couple of bottles from underneath her display table. She showed them to me. One was full, the other almost gone. Both of them had her name written in black marker. "I love them. Since I bring them with me, I put my name on them because I don't want to send anyone home with used bottles."

She unscrewed the top of the one almost gone and rolled it on the insides of her wrist before she tossed it in the trashcan behind her.

"Makes me calm." Her mouth twisted wryly. "I don't have anyone but me to rely on. And this is just a side hustle to get me out of some debt while I've got a lot of resumes out there. But truly, I've made six-figures in the last month doing a little home party here and there, so I'm not sure if I'll take a job if offered."

"Well, you're doing great. One day, you just might have a shop like mine. You know…," I tapped my temples as I tried to wrap my head around the number she just told me she'd made. "Darla. . .um . . .my mother, she did this like you. Is there still a flea market in Locust Grove?"

"I think so," she said and began to put all of my purchases into a used Piggly Wiggly plastic grocery bag.

"Why don't you rent a space there and sell these?" I asked. "Darla did it and that's how we lived."

"Your mom?" She asked, and I nodded. "Why do you call her Darla and not mom?"

My lips broke into a wide-open smile and I rolled my eyes, finding myself shaking my head from the truly fond memory.

"Darla was very interesting. She didn't like to be called mom. She always made sure everyone knew she was my mother, but she liked to be called by her name. It was her thing." There was a good feeling inside of me that let me carry on Darla's passion and actually help people.

"That's a wonderful idea." She grabbed a pad of paper and wrote something down. "Do you have any other tips?"

"Maybe you should do some sort of incentive for people with businesses to put these in their shop instead of begging people, like you did Leah," I said then whispered, *though you don't need the sales with the money you made, under my breath.*

I found myself feeling sorry for her. In fact, I saw a little bit of myself in Gabby or maybe it was a piece of Darla. Either way, she was harmless. A few pointers wouldn't hurt and if I could get her out of Whispering Falls, maybe business would pick up.

Then I opened my big mouth, "My friend owns the Piggly Wiggly. I can't promise anything, but I'm having supper with her tonight. What if I give her your business card? She likes to showcase local business."

Gabby squealed and rushed over, throwing her arms around me, giving me a big hug.

"Thank you!" She continued to bounce on the balls of her feet while clapping her hands in delight. "Here." She darted back over to her display and handed me a couple of her business cards.

"I'm not promising anything." I had to make sure she understood.

"Don't worry. Anything helps. I'm all out of the Breathe, so I'll have to drop it off tomorrow or the next day." She handed me the bag full of the plain bottles that hurt my soul. "That'll be five hundred dollars."

With my hands full of the fake oils and my treats from Wicked Good, I trekked up the hill to my house.

I lived behind A Charming Cure. It had a wonderful hillside view of Whispering Falls and all the quaint shops. The sun was starting to stay out longer and the last rays of the day dripped over the village. The problem with the days being longer was that we had to wait until the full moon for the smudge ceremony. There was just enough time to host my dinner party between now and the time for the ceremony.

There was a magical layer that hung over all of the shops' awnings and lit up all the ornamental gates in the most amazing rainbow. A clap of thunder and hint of danger shocked me out of my trance. My bag warmed against my leg. I gripped the bag of oils and dessert so I wouldn't drop it. My intuition was in full force. Something was brewing and it wasn't good.

A big wave of black started from Glorybee Pet Store and rolled over the shops, stopping shy of Crazy Crafty Chick. My eyes blinked a few times. On the last blink, the magical layer had returned to the village.

"There you are." The door to my house swept opened and Oscar stood there. "We wondered where you were."

Rowl, rowl. Mr. Prince Charming rolled himself in front of my feet, giving his back a good scratch.

I handed Oscar all the bags and bent down to pick up my ornery cat.

"Are you okay?" Oscar's blue eyes had a deep-set worry.

"I'm fine." Not necessarily the truth, but I was fine with him and Mr. Prince Charming. I ruffled the top of his black hair as I walked past him and into the house. "Chandra get a hold of you?"

"She did. She was hanging out of Cleansing Spirit Spa while someone was waiting for their nails to dry. She said I needed a haircut." He followed me inside and put the bags on the table.

Mr. Prince Charming jumped out of my arms and scurried over to the orange couch so he could perch on the back and stare out the window.

"It looks great." I kissed him on the lips and then took my bag off my shoulder, hanging it on the back of the kitchen chair.

Our house was a small one bedroom with one bath, kitchen and family room combination that was perfect for us. I was born here. This was my parents' house, so when I moved back to Whispering Falls, Bella Von Low had been caretaker after all of those years. She simply handed the keys over to me.

"What on earth is all this?" He looked into the grocery bag and pulled out one of the bottles. "I don't have to use my wizard powers to know this isn't real." He unscrewed the small metal top and took a whiff. "Did you buy this?"

"I did. I felt bad for this girl. She reminded me of Darla and maybe a bit of myself." I walked over to the fireplace and gathered my matches. "I'll tell you and everyone else about it over supper."

"It better be a good story." He outstretched his arms for me to curl in to before we headed into the kitchen to prepare for our guests.

Chapter Six

"Come in," I chimed. When I opened the door, Eloise Sandlewood was standing there.

She'd been a mother figure to Oscar since his parents had passed to the Great Beyond like my own. She was his aunt. It was amazing how she stepped up to the plate after Oscar and I had moved to Whispering Falls and discovered their family connection.

Sure, she knew it all along, but we had to discover our own path. When it was revealed she was his aunt, it was like they'd known each other all of their lives.

"I brought you the first batch of Singing Neetles." She pulled out the most color batch of Darla's favorite flower from underneath her long red cape. The color matched her short red hair perfectly and made her emerald eyes pop.

Eloise was what we called a Fairiwick. She was part fairy and part spiritualist. She had the gift of incents. She was able to sense danger which gave her the job of doing a morning cleanse in the precious space of time between dark and before dawn. There was a small window during the morning where she walked the main street of the village and cleansed the entire town.

Some mornings I would watch her from the kitchen window. It was a beautiful ceremony and I would sip my coffee as I enjoyed the show.

"Thank you," I tried to answer over the low hum of the boutique of flowers.

"It's about their bedtime, so they'll settle down soon." She winked referring to the flowers since they hummed and sung cheery tunes all day. It was something only spiritualist could hear and Chandra Shango had them planted in the window boxes of Cleansing Spirit Spa.

They sang all day long, echoing over the hills of Whispering Falls. They always lifted our spirits. Darla loved the colors and I really wished she was able to hear them, but since she was a mortal, she couldn't. I knew she knew they were special,however. Maybe my dad had told her about them, at least that's what I told myself because they hadn't had any secrets between them.

"It's going to be a fine night for a smudge." She stepped into the house and twirled out of her cape. It floated over to the coat stand and found a hook. She used the tips of her fingernails to fluff up her pixie cut hair.

"Aunt Eloise." Oscar came from the kitchen and greeted her with a cocktail. "We are so glad you and Adeline could come for supper."

"I hope you don't mind I invited my mortal friend Adeline from Locust Grove." I couldn't remember if I'd told her. "She needed to make a trip into Whispering Falls to get a new supply of potions, um. . .lotions." I winked because that's how I marketed them to customers.

Some of my potions had gotten in the mortal bath and body industry. Those sales channels were going great, but it was the shop that had my heart because it was Darla's that I wanted to make sure went well. Once word got out about how well my lotions made mortals feel, I'd gotten a big contract with a very popular body lotion chain and a few stores like the Piggly Wiggly in Locust Grove.

"I don't mind at all. She's lovely." Aunt Eloise gave me a quick kiss on each cheek and headed into the kitchen to help Oscar cook.

I wasn't the best in the kitchen. In fact, I was horrible. Oscar was amazing and didn't even use his wizard magic to help.

In the distance, I could see Adeline's car pulling up the driveway. I stood at the door waiting for her as she parked next to The Green Machine, what I lovingly called my old, green El Camino that I couldn't part with.

"I'm so happy to be here." Adeline's big smile was a much-needed breath of fresh air. She had her sandy blond hair pulled up in a top-knot on top of her head, making her features stand out. She was such a lovely woman on the inside and outside.

She had been my biggest customer since the beginning. If I had stayed in Locust Grove, I'm sure we'd been inseparable. I'd even classify her as a sister.

"I've missed you so much." I gave her a great big hug, making sure not to crush her tiny frame. "I can't believe I have to bribe you with a home cooked Oscar meal to get you here."

"I'm here for the goods." She joked and headed into the house. "Hey, there," she called over to Oscar and Eloise, as she walked straight over to the couch and picked up Mr. Prince Charming.

His purr was so loud, I was sure people in Locust Grove could hear his happy heart.

"I've missed my snuggles from you," Adeline spoke baby talk to him.

"Please stop," Oscar snarled from the kitchen in a joking manner, though I knew better.

He and Mr. Prince Charming had that love hate relationship where both of them wanted to keep me safe, so they fought over it on a regular basis. I wasn't willing to get rid of either, which meant they were just going to suck it up and get along.

"He's so smushy and warm." She curled him even more into her arms.

"There's no use," I told Oscar. "He's got her heart."

"Look what June brought home in that bag on the table." Oscar pointed to the Piggly Wiggly bag.

"From the Piggly?" Leah asked and put Mr. Prince Charming back on the couch.

He didn't stay there. He jumped off the couch and was under her foot the entire time.

"No. There was a girl that is doing the Lifestyle oil parties and I bought some." I walked over to the table and began to take out the oils one at a time. "Oh no." I gasped when I saw the one that had Gabby written on it. "This belongs to the girl. I need to put this in my bag and give to Leah."

Immediately, I grabbed my bag off the back of the chair and stuck it in there so I wouldn't forget or worse, use it.

"Why on earth did you buy all of these when they aren't. . ." Eloise's eye drew down her nose and she glanced over at Adeline. "yours?" She finished, though I knew she meant magical.

"They are a bit plain and not like your amazing bottles but I have heard of them." Adeline picked them up and opened each, taking them to her nose and smelling them.

"I just wanted to take a look at them and see if they worked. That's all." I took the business card out of the bag and handed it to Adeline. "I told her I'd give you her card in case you wanted to showcase her as a local business, but she's making six figures with this stuff."

"A Charming Cure has been losing customers and sales. We think it's because of these home oil parties popping up." Oscar didn't waste any time getting to the root of the matter.

"June, they can't hold a candle to yours." Eloise scolded me. "I can't believe you wasted money on these imposters."

"I don't know." Adeline held a bottle with the price facing Eloise. "The hardest part of selling one of June's product at the Piggly Wiggly is the cost. This is half of the cost."

Eloise opened her mouth to protest.

"But." Adeline stopped Eloise from talking as she put up her finger. "When I tell them to try June's product, they forget all about the cost and it's a sale."

That was because I'd made a special potion for the retail outlets. I'd come up with a formula that was specific to what the customer was looking for. Inside the lotion was an active spell ingredient that read the customer's needs like I did when they were in front of me at the shop, making the lotion magically evolve into the spell the customer needed. It was the perfect way to specialize the lotion without actually having them in the shop.

"I make sure to keep an employee at her display all day long so we don't miss out on a customer." Adeline had been such a great friend and businesswoman to work with. She really knew her stuff.

"Trust me when I say that business will pick up. I can feel it." Eloise curled a fist to her chest. "I can really feel it's going to be…soon."

The way she said soon was as dramatic as the lift in her brows when she said it. My mouth went dry, the room tilted left and right. I grabbed the edge of the kitchen table to steady myself, taking some really deep breaths. As much as

I wanted to smell the delicious food Oscar was making, the scents of Geranium, Fennel, Carrot Seed, Palmarosa, and Vitex took a dive down my nose and into my soul. Making my senses and intuition perk to life like a live wire.

Chapter Seven

On the way down the hill to A Charming Cure to get the tools needed for the smudging ceremony, I glanced around the village to see if that wave of darkness had returned. Though I was doing a smudge to welcome in the full summer season, a little added protection from what I'd seen earlier wouldn't hurt.

The carriage lights that were dotted along the main street glowed. Arabella Paxton stood on a ladder at the base of one of the lampposts. She appeared to be stretched to her limits with one arm holding on and the other trying to hook a beautiful flower arrangement on a rod.

"Here." I placed my hands on the ladder to steady it. "Give me the hanging basket. When you get up there, I'll hand it to you."

"You're a lifesaver." She smiled with gratitude, her ice blue eyes melting into her high cheekbones.

Carefully, I grabbed the hook off the basket and kept ahold of the ladder with my other hand. Arabella was much steadier using two hands to climb. Once at the rung she needed to be at, she held her arm out, extending her hand.

"These are so pretty," I said and lifted it up to her.

"Begonias, Lobelia, and Million Bells can make any arrangement beautiful this time of the year. Plus, donating these to the village helps get my name out there." She referred to Magical Moments, her flower shop. "Oh, poo." She looked down and around the ladder. "Do you mind terribly to run into my shop and grab the wire snips? I've got to make an adjustment to the baskets and I thought I had them."

"I don't mind at all." I shook the ladder slightly to make sure she was stable. "You okay up there?"

"I'll be fine." She nodded. Her long black hair flowed down her back. "They are probably just inside the door," she called after me.

The front gate of Magical Moments was amazing. Instead of plain wrought iron, the slats were made to look like long-stemmed flowers with the blossoms on the top. When the gate was touched, the iron rods turned green like a flower's stem and the top of each one blossomed a different colored flower. Arabella told her customers that it was sorta like one of those childhood mood rings.

The babbling water from the small creek that ran right through the middle of her shop was soothing to my soul. I stood inside of the door taking big, deep breaths. The aroma of fresh flowers, moss, and wet soil circled around me. The wire snips were exactly where she said they'd be. I bent down to pick them up just as a butterfly darted past my nose.

I watched as the beautiful orange and black creature dipped and floated a few times until it rested on one of the living flowerbeds alongside of the creek. It was amazing how beautiful and inviting Arabella had made the shop.

Customers could walk along each side of the creek by walking over a small, wooden bridge. She'd displayed her arrangements on tiered black tables with lines of black vases filled with all sorts of bright and colorful flowers.

Many times, if I needed a special flower for a cure, Arabella was able to provide my request. It was wonderful.

The butterfly floated by again, bringing me back to the present. I squeezed the wire snips in my hand and rushed back out of the shop.

"I'm so sorry." I lifted my hand up in the air and gave Arabella the snips. "I get lost in your shop every time I go in there. Like a little spa. But don't tell Chandra I said that."

"Don't tell Chandra what?" Chandra had big ears. She loved to gossip and she just so happened to walk up on us.

"I must confess." I drew my hands together. "I told Arabella her shop rejuvenated me like a spa."

"I'm going to have to agree with you." Chandra smiled. "Are you ready for the ceremony?" She looked up as a big dark cloud covered a fourth of the moon.

"After I get her off this ladder, I have to run into my shop to grab my things."

Chandra used her hip to bump me out of the way.

"I've got it. You go and get the stuff. There's a good episode of Bewitched on tonight. You know the one where Darrin meets Endora for the first time." She giggled, shaking her whole body.

"How many times have you seen that one?" I asked and let her take my stance at the bottom of the ladder while Arabella snipped away at the hanging basket.

"Go on," she instructed and nodded towards A Charming Cure.

"See y'all soon." I gave a full hand finger wave and continued down the street, only a shop down really.

Between A Charming Cure and Magical Moments, my longtime friend and Native American, KJ opened a much-needed herb shop. The lights in his shop were already off.. I looked up and down the street, noticing all the shops had turned out their lights which meant they were probably under the moon at the Gathering Rock waiting on me. I really wanted to return that bottle of Gabby's oil to Leah, but it'd have to wait until after the smudge.

I hurried through my gate, up the steps to the shop, and quickly unlocked the door with my skeleton key. Without much thinking, I flipped on the light switch.

Meow, mewl! Mr. Prince Charming was sitting on the counter.

"How did you get in here?" I asked him.

It was a completely stupid question because he couldn't answer me and I'd never figured out how he'd gotten into different places that required a key.

He walked along the edge of the counter and dragged his tail to the back wall where I kept all my bottles of herbs.

"You are trying to tell me something." I bit my lip and eyed him to try and figure out what he was doing. "When you know what you want me to know, tell me."

I went ahead and gathered the supplies I needed. When I went behind the partition to retrieve the Magical Cures Book that Darla had left for me, I noticed the cauldron was on. There was a purple substance with a ribbon of light purple swirling in its depth.

"Mr. Prince Charming, did you turn on my cauldron?" I asked and peeked out from behind the partition.

He was teetering on the edge of the counter with his tail stiff and pointing directly at the bottle of black cumin seeds. The white ceramic jar fit perfectly in the palm of a hand and had little red dotted shaped diamonds all over the bottle. The clear glass cork top glowed with a vibrant purple. It was a sure sign that it was to be used by me in some sort of capacity.

"If you say so." I reached up and picked up the bottle. In normal circumstances, and for a customer, I would drag my finger along the shelf of herbs and when the bottle lit up, that's how I knew it was to be used in that customer's cure. Not tonight. Apparently, I was to use it during the smudge ceremony.

This was a first for me. Mr. Prince Charming rarely aided in the ingredients of a potion. After I took it off the shelf, he returned to himself, using his paw to make two quick swipes in the air before he jumped down and darted under a table.

The cauldron had turned a lighter shade of purple and was bubbling. Carefully, I uncorked the top of the seeds and sprinkled a dash of them in the bubbling mixture. The light purple moved into a swirl of pink with red accretions that lay on the top. A strange mix of Geranium, Fennel, Carrot Seed, Palmarosa, and Vitex floated and curled up in a puff of smoke above the raging cauldron.

I took a step back and lifted my hands overtop the cauldron, letting the smoke cover them fully so I could deliver the spell intended for the smudge ceremony.

I closed my eyes and let the words that'd formed in my gut pull through my soul and out my mouth, "Protect from the Eye which has looked on me or the village for harm. Protect with light that is pure and loving. I reject the Evil Eye. Hand of Fatima, send it away from me."

There was a loud crack of fireworks over the cauldron before it shut off and my hands dropped. I brought my hands close to my face and noticed the glow around them. As though I didn't have control over them, they floated over top of the Magical Cures Book.

The cover flipped opened and the pages were turning so fast, my short black hair blew behind my ears. It was as though I was in an air tunnel and then it suddenly stopped, arms dropping to my side, rendering me breathless.

I stood there for a minute to let my breathing come back to normal and my eyes refocus. My fingers tingled as if they'd been asleep. I took a couple of steps forward to read the page the book opened to. The ink was invisible ink but had now come to life on the page.

Before I knew I was a spiritualist and had my "gift", I would open the book and it would appear to be just a bunch of jibber-jabberish writing. When I accepted my spiritual gift, it was only then that I could see clearly the pages; what I'd considered to be a journal that Darla had kept all my life. It was a priceless and precious gift.

"Not that I feel in danger, but I always feel someone is watching me and June," I read Darla's scribble on the page. "There is an evil lurking. I wished my husband was here. He'd know what to do. But since he is not, I must go to my shed and create my own protection spell."

"Evil Eye of Protection," I read the headlines of the spell as the picture of a hand with a triangle with an eye in the middle of it appeared faintly in the background of the page.

As I read what I needed to perform the ceremony, I grabbed my smudge bag and added all the stuff I needed for this one. It wasn't too much off of the protection spell I'd always tried to incorporate during the smudge.

I grabbed a bundle of general smudge sticks and carefully dipped them into the cauldron. As soon as I pulled the bundle out of the mixture, it instantly dried and withered, making it perfect for burning.

"Let's go," I told Mr. Prince Charming on my way past the display table where he was hiding. I held the door for him to run past me and flipped the lights off , making sure the door was locked before I stepped out and shut it behind us.

Chapter Eight

The smudging ceremony took place in the woods up the hill from the village. Just beyond the tree line was a clear space with a big rock in the front. Before I even made it up the hill and past the trees, I could hear the murmur of the spiritualists from the village that were already gathered there.

When they saw me, they all parted to make room as I walked into the circle and up to the rock. Leah was standing to the far right of the rock, so on my way over, I took the bottle of oil out of my bag.

"Gabby accidentally gave me her personal bottle of oil. Do you mind returning it to her?" I asked Leah, placing the small bottle in the palm of her hand and using my hand to curl her fingers around it.

A jolt of electricity shocked my fingers, giving me sadness in my soul. I tried not to look too much into my intuition to see what was coming from Leah, but something deep rooted was there when I mention Gabby.

"Are you okay?" I asked her and dropped my hand.

"I'm great. I'll be more than happy to return it to her," she said, not giving me permission, per the by-laws, to get any insight to what I'd felt from her.

Ignoring my intuition, I headed over to the rock and sat my bag on the ground and opened it, taking out the smudge bundle I'd dipped into the cauldron, an eagle feather, and matches. I placed them on top of the rock. I'm not real sure what that signified, but there was some sort of significance to the ritual and it'd always been performed this way. The rock was special to the community and at any time if one of us needed a little rejuvenating, we could come to the rock and just sit. Not that we worshiped it, but I liked to believe that the rock had a clear path to be bathed in the sun and moon, giving it positive properties. Not to mention, it was quiet and remote, just a good place to get away and relax.

The spiritualists had gathered into a circle by the time I'd turned around. I walked into the middle and gave every one of them eye contact as my eyes made their way around the circle. After I did this, I walked back to the rock and picked up the smudge stick to light it. Once lit, I ran the smoldering stick up and down my body, letting the smoke circle around me for protection.

With the feather in my hand, I walked around the back side from spiritualist to spiritualist, using the feather in an upward curling motion to fan the smoke up and down them. Without having to even remember the words that formed on my lips in the shop, they floated out of my mouth like the smoke floated up into the pitch-black night above our heads, absorbed into the rays of the full moon.

"Protect from the Eye which has looked on me or the village for harm. Protect with light that is pure and loving. I reject the Evil Eye. Hand of Fatima, send it away from me," I whispered to each spiritualist as I fanned the feather along their backside.

After I'd completed the same ceremony and said the same words to their front side, the smudge stick stopped smoking. It was then that I knew the spell had taken hold and it was time to bury it.

I glanced over at KJ. He was tall with dark eyes and dark skin. He was a beautiful man on the inside and out. He was dressed in a loincloth and headdress with the exact eagle feathers weaved into his braided black hair.

His eyes met mine. He stepped forward and took one step on his right foot before he started to chant in his native tongue, dancing his way over to the middle of the circle where I put the smudge stick on the ground.

I walked between Oscar and Colton Lance, the other sheriff of Whispering Falls, and clasped hands. As KJ did his spiritual dance and used his hands to bury the smudge stick, the circle of hands lifted high in the air as the protection spell was returned back to the earth.

After the air cleared and KJ had returned to the circle, everyone dropped their hands and went back to socializing.

"How did you like the Lifestyle party?" Izzy swept up to me. Her long lashes batted.

"It was fine. I know that it's a bunch of oils and herbs put together that do have some effect on moods and hormones, but not a full cure like I make." I smiled, and continued, "I just hope business picks up."

"It will. With the summer coming and the tourists out and about, they all come back each year. Gabby is just getting clients that live around here." Izzy made a good point. "You know that I'd never let anything happen to your shop."

Izzy had been the president of the village for a long time and she was the one who had encouraged me and Oscar to move here. She knew who we were all along and that's how Mr. Prince Charming came to live with me. It was his job to report back to her if I had developed any spiritual powers. Plus, Mr. McGurtle, our nosey neighbor in Locust Grove, was put there to keep a human eye on me. I thought he was just being super nosey when I'd catch him in the shrubbery looking over at me and Darla with his binoculars. He was taking good notes and reporting back to the village council as they tried to decide how to get me back to Whispering Falls to fulfill my destiny.

She was right. She always did right by me and I believed her.

"Thank you." I reached out, took her by the hand and squeezed it.

"I've seen a definite uptake in all the shops." She nodded and put her hands together in Namaste pose. "The balls are streaming with happy and light."

She referred to her shop, Mystic Lights, which was a lighting shop with unique lamps and shades as well as crystal balls. It was her cover for her spiritual gift of crystal ball reading.

Years ago, when I first walked into her shop, Madame Torres started to roll and rumble and mumble when I walked past her. I didn't know I was a spiritualist and felt like I was seeing things. Little did I know how crystal balls could spend years in silence until they found their spiritualist. Madame Torres had been waiting for me all her life and she's not shut up since.

"Are you ready to go home?" Oscar walked up and put his arm around me. "It's getting late."

Me, Oscar, and Izzy looked up at the moon.

"Yes. I feel like we are going to have a busy day tomorrow." Izzy's eyes drew down. The moonlight rays hit her lashes, drawing a long shadow down her cheeks.

They continued to say their goodbyes and I looked back up at the moon that suddenly had deep purple waves running through it.

"You're going to need this." Bella slipped my charm bracelet back on my wrist, her eyes had a purple tint to them.

Goosebumps covered my body.

Chapter Nine

"June. June. Juuuunnnneeee," Madame Torres sang in the middle of the night pulling me out of a deep slumber.

"Not now." I tapped her on top of her globe.

"June Heal, there's a message for you." Her words were muffled.

I turned my head. Her head was floating in the black water,lips painted red, eyes big with bright yellow eye shadow upon them. I blinked a few times to stir my foggy head.

"Look deep into the depths of the raging water to see. It'll be me you seek and be. The mix of smells will bring you closure, but not until a few days will be over." Madame Torres lit up with a vibrant white light, waking me.

"What? What did you say?" I sat up and grabbed her, bringing the ball up to my face.

"If you'd listen to me like you're supposed to, then we wouldn't have to waste time doing redos." Her nose snarled. I glared at her. "Fine. Turn on your listening ears." She huffed.

"Just repeat what you said." I held her close to my face and ignored Mr. Prince Charming's pawing between me and my cranky crystal ball, Madame Torres.

Oscar mumbled something and flipped over, going right back to sleep.

With Madame Torres in my grip, I pulled the cover back then dangled my legs over the side of the bed. My toes tapped around the floor until they found my comfy slippers. Even though the weather was turning much warmer, the mornings were still chilly and it was early. Very early.

Mr. Prince Charming had darted off the bed and out the door. I followed him and flipped on the lights in the kitchen, as well as the coffee pot.

I sat down in a kitchen chair to wait for the pot to brew, sitting Madame Torres on the table.

"Divine light of the full moon, speak to me the truth." I circled my hands over Madame Torres. If she wasn't going to just tell me what I needed to know, I was going to go old school and force her to talk to me. "The truth you tell will determine the spell."

"Fine." Her face appeared. "I said, look deep into the depths of the raging water to see. It'll be me you seek and be. The mix of smells will bring you closure, but not until a few days will be over."

"What does that mean?" I looked deep into the ball and tried to see beyond her big noggin'. There were a few bottles floating around. "Are those Gabby's bottles?"

"All I know is what I bring from the spirits. It's up to you to determine the worth." She wasn't very forthcoming with her information.

Rowl, rowl! Mr. Prince Charming stood up on his hind legs next to the counter and batted the air.

"What's wrong?" I stood up and walked over to him, but he'd already jumped up on the counter and smacked the charm bracelet onto the ground. "I guess I need to put that on."

I bent down and picked up the bracelet. I ran my finger along the charms. There was the small turtle charm, an owl, purple stone in mesh, angel wing, dove sitting on a gold circle, third eye charm, small potion bottle, a brass bell, a spiral silver charm, a leaf, and now the hand of Fatima. Each of one of them held a significant meaning to the stages in my life as a spiritualist and just how important my job was to the world. I held the bracelet in my hand and took a deep breath. My intuition flipped on my creative juices.

Mr. Prince Charming must've felt it too. He walked back and forth on the edge of the counter, dragging the tip of his tail underneath my nose.

"You are so silly." I itched my nose and quickly clipped on the bracelet.

The coffee pot beeped letting me know the brew was ready. I grabbed a mug out of the cabinet and poured a hot, steaming cup. My hip leaned into the counter as I kept both hands wrapped around the warm coffee, staring out the window and down the hill.

The beginning of a smile tipped the corners of my mouth when I saw the faint glow of Eloise's incense burner fling forward and back. I closed my eyes and listened. In the distance I could hear the faint sound of the chain attached to the burner as she flung it out and back in.

I lifted the cup of coffee and took sips, watching her do the ritual cleansing.

"Mmmm…yes…" Madame Torres came back to life. "The mix of smells will bring you closure, but not until a few days will be over."

There was a sudden shift in the spiritual world. The air thickened, the village tilted. The clink of Eloise's chain stopped and replaced by the sounds of Two Sisters and A Funeral ambulance siren.

"Oscar, get up." I hurried back down the hall, flipping on every light in the house.

I slipped on my pair of jeans and a sweater.

"Oscar, get up! Something is wrong." I didn't have time to dilly-dally.

"What?" Oscar sat up. His hair was a little ruffled up. His eyes were sleepy. Before he could ask any questions, his cell went off.

I didn't bother waiting around to see what or who it was. I already knew that it was either his aunt or Colton letting him know that something was going on.

With my bag strapped over my shoulder, I opened the door. Mr. Prince Charming darted out of the house and down the hill. I ran behind him, knowing he'd lead me right to whatever was going on.

I wasn't sure, but I knew in my gut that it wasn't good.

The Karima's old time ambulance had parked in the middle of the street between KJ's store and Leah's shop.

Their little red light was swirling in the glass globe from on top of their car.

Colton, Eloise, Patience and Constance were huddled on the side walk in front of one of the carriage lights.

"What's going on?" I asked.

"I told you I smelled death." A melancholy frown flitted across Patience Karima's features.

"Mmmhhhmmmm. Death." Constance nodded with a critical squint as she took a step back.

"Gabby?" I gasped. "Is she?"

"She's dead." Colton pulled his fingers from her neck, and looked up at me.

The cloud moved from in front of the moon. A ray darted down from the sky and shined a spotlight on Gabby's hand. Like it was water to a wilted flower, her hand uncurled and the bottle I'd given Leah rolled out.

Chapter Ten

"I was just doing my normal cleansing," Eloise told Oscar after he'd started to question her about what she saw.

Colton Lance, also a wizard, was going over the crime scene with his wand. The bottle that'd fallen out of Gabby's grip floated into the air and found it a home in an evidence bag.

Eloise was shaking, still holding on to the incense burner with the chains dangling by her side. They rattled along with her nerves. She looked between me and Oscar with her big emerald eyes. "I knew something was off this morning when I got here, and the teenagers were buzzing around."

"The teenagers were here?" I wondered what they'd seen.

The teenagers were actually Lightning Bugs. Unfortunately, they'd passed in the real world far too soon and came back as Lightning Bugs. True to the nature of the insect, up all night and sleeps all day was the perfect animal for them to come back as. They were pretty vigilant.

"Yes. I was at home and they were there in swarms. They did circles until I got the incense ready. Then they made a beeline to the village. Once we were here, they disappeared." Her brows dipped as if she were confused. "I looked all over for them, but they were gone. I continued to do the cleanse. I do two cleanses at dawn and I was on the second one when she appeared out of nowhere."

"What do you mean appeared?" Oscar asked.

"Her body was just lying right here, and it wasn't there before." She nodded and pointed to where Gabby was still on the ground. "I practically tripped over her feet. I'm telling you she wasn't there the first time." She slid her eyes up the carriage light pole. "I even stopped at every light the first time to bless the beautiful flowers Adeline had hung."

"Coming through. Move it. Coming through." I heard Constance Karima's words but the rickety sound of the Two Sisters and a Funeral's church cart rattling was what announced that death had come upon us.

"Make sure Colton is finished before you take her body." Oscar told them. "I'll be by later to get some preliminary results."

"Yes, sir." Constance and Patience Karima stood ramrod straight with right hand saluted and then continued to do their job while Oscar focused again on his aunt.

"Did you hear anything?" He asked Eloise.

She curled the long red cape up around her chin with one hand while the other continued to hold the burner.

"The incense." She pulled the lantern up to her face. "It wouldn't light on the second round. It was the strangest thing." Her jaw dropped as if she suddenly remembered something. "I rushed back to my house to get a new burner between the two cleanses." She dropped the cape with her hand and brought it up to her forehead. "I can't believe I forgot that."

"It's okay. You're shaken up and it's normal to forget things." Oscar was such a good nephew. He hugged her. "I want you to go home and get some rest. Most times, your memory will come back to you after you've distanced yourself for a little bit. If you do remember something, let me know."

"Okay," she sighed a bit of relief. Her jaw softened. "I'm going to go now."

"I'll check in on you later." I gave her a hug. Within seconds, she'd disappeared behind the village.

"Too bad she wasn't a spiritualist." Petunia shrugged and held a small tray of muffins from The Gathering Grove in one hand and continued to bounce on the balls of her feet.

Orin, her one year old baby with Gerald, was fast asleep in the baby carrier strapped on her back.

Her messy up-do was teetering on top of her head and stopped once the bird that was perched inside popped its head out. She fed it a piece of muffin.

"Try one. They are so good." She pushed the tray closer to me.

I took one and so did most of the others as she offered them.

"If she were a spiritualist, that'd mean someone from our world had come under attack. I'm glad she wasn't." I bit down into the warm and soft muffin. It was not June's Gem, but it did help a smidgen.

"If she were, then maybe she'd been able to come back and I'd been able to help." Petunia let out a long audible breath as we watched Colton give the Karima sisters the go ahead to take Gabby to the morgue.

"I'm going to have to act fast on this one since she is a mortal." Petunia Shrubwood was the village president and animal spiritualist. Most times when a spiritualist had passed to the next life, they usually came back as an animal that represented their previous life.

If they were a bad-sider, which was more along the side of an evil spiritualist. Their focus was to harm using their gift, but not all were evil and some did nice things. Then we had the good-siders, like our village. We all helped everyone out in times of need. We might not all agree on all things, but that was normal.

As a matter of fact, Eloise was considered a bad-sider because she was a fairy-wick and not of a pure breed like me or Oscar. They weren't able to live in the village limits and that's why she lived deep in the woods.

"The mortals will hear about this and I hope it doesn't hurt the sales and the tourist traffic." Petunia shook her head and a few dead leaves dropped out of her hair, fluttering to the ground. "I must go and get this all figured out."

"I'm sure you'll have a good statement for the mortal papers." I assured her and reached out to squeeze her forearm.

"Thank you, June. Now, I've got to get Orin to the sitter so I can get to work." She shook her head. "Stop by later."

"I will." I tried to smile, but my eyes caught the Karimas putting the white sheet up over Gabby's head before they pulled the church cart up and locked it in place.

"I can't believe this." I whispered to myself and gulped back tears. I watched Oscar and Colton collect evidence and snap photos of the crime scene while the Karimas adjusted Gabby.

"I can't either." Leah said in low, cracked southern voice.

"Leah," I gasped, not realizing she'd walked up next to me. "What happened?" I asked tugging her elbow to follow me across the street so no one could hear us.

"What do you mean?" She asked.

"I gave you that bottle of Gabby's last night. Did you give it to her?" I asked.

"I went to my shop last night after the smudge. She was still there. I wasn't sure why she hadn't left yet." Her blue eyes were blurred behind the wall of tears that'd been built up in her eyes. She blinked, sending a few tears down her cheeks. "She wasn't able to give me an explanation. She said that she was doing business."

"Business?" That struck me as an odd thing for Gabby to have said. "I thought the party was over at 6 p.m."

"It was. Right before you came back, she said she was going to pack up. Then I left the room when you came in.

The next thing I know, she was on her phone fussing with someone and she wrote down on a piece of paper that she'd lock up the shop after I tried to hurry her out."

"Why didn't you wait for her to leave?" My intuition started to ping me that this didn't look good for Leah.

"I didn't want to be late for the smudge ceremony. I'm new and I really wanted to make a good impression." The edges of her lips dipped. "It's in my southern roots not to be late to anything."

"This would've been one time that you should've." I watched Patience Karima rush over to the ambulance and open the double back doors. "What did you say when you saw her after the smudge?"

"I told her that she had to leave." She snapped her fingers, her eyes widened, and her mouth formed an "O". "She said that she was waiting for someone."

"Did she say who?" I asked. "If you know, that might be who killed her."

"Killed her?" Leah drew back.

"I mean. . ." I bit my lip.

"You mean murdered. That's what you mean," Leah's voice carried through in a loud echo since Whispering Falls was set in a holler. It was easy to do.

A hushed whisper blanketed the crowd and all eyes seem to have turned to look across the street at us.

"Murder?" the word swept across the lips of all the spiritualists that'd gathered to see what was going on as the orange and red colors brought the dawn of day.

Oscar's blue eyes pierced the distance between us. It wasn't in an approving way.

Chapter Eleven

"Here, yea, here, yea," Faith Mortimer's voice sat on the light breeze that floated through Whispering Falls as the spiritual newspaper was delivered. *"There has been a tragic death that has fallen upon our village. Gabby Summerfield, a mortal that sold Lifestyle oils as recent as last night at Crazy Crafty Chick Shop, was found this morning while Eloise Sandlewood was cleansing the village. If you are waiting for an order of the Lifestyle oils, please see Leah LeRoy for details. It did slip out of Intuitionist June Heal, owner of A Charming Cure, that Gabby had been murdered."*

A long-exhausted sigh escaped my lips as I took my skeleton key out of my bag and stepped up on the top step of A Charming Cure. Oscar wasn't going to like this at all.

"In other news. . ."

Her words ran together, and I zoned out as I unlocked the door of A Charming Cure.

"Today's news was brought to you by Glorybee Pet Store. Stop by and see Petunia for all of your pets needs."

I ran my hand up along the wall and flipped on the lights once I was inside. Mr. Prince Charming rushed in under my feet. There was a table just inside the door with a cute cauldron I put some warm tea in during the day along with plastic cups where the customers could help themselves. *Compliments of The Gathering Grove*. The sweet treats were there for the taking courtesy of Wicked Good Bakery.

"There you are." I felt a little more at ease knowing he was there. "Gabby was murdered wasn't she?" I flipped the OPEN sign.

Meow, meow. Mr. Prince Charming jumped from display table to display table next to me as I made my way to the counter.

I took off the bag strapped across my body and hung it on the back of the chair. I dug my hand inside and took out Madame Torres, putting her on the counter. If she had something to say during the work day, I knew I couldn't afford to miss out.

Mr. Prince Charming took the opportunity to give her a good smack when he jumped up on the counter.

"Stop it," Madame Torres spat from a clear ball. "You aren't the most valuable guide for June. All you can say is meow, mewl," she mocked him.

He continued to bat her and drag his claws down the side.

"Meow kitty, kitty." She let out a ruckus laugh and sent a loud clap of thunder.

The fur on the back of his neck stood up and he darted off the counter, finding a good hiding space under a table.

"Scaredy-cat!" Madame Torres laugh became scornful.

"That's enough you two." I reprimanded them on a regular basis. They continually fought over whom I relied on most. "Both of you bring something different to my gift," I reminded them before I disappeared behind the partition and flipped on the cauldron.

While the cauldron warmed, I made the changes to the blackboard, but not alone. The chalk had a mind of its own. Geranium, Fennel, Carrot Seed, Palmarosa, and Vitex, the chalk scribbled.

"She said something about smells." My head jerked to Madame Torres as I remembered what she'd said this morning while I was waking from that restful sleep. "Oh on," I searched my memory. "What did she say?" I took in a deep breath to calm myself. My mind was a jumble and my insides were a wreck. "You told me something about smells." I leaned over top her at the counter. "What did you say again?" I asked the clear ball, but she was nowhere to be found.

The lights flickered, and a tornado of wind whipped up in the middle of the shop in a narrow funnel from the ground to the ceiling. My blunt bangs flew back from the burst of wind.

Hiss, hiss. Mr. Prince Charming wasn't as happy as I was with the arrival of our guest.

The welcomed small burst of energy was the arrival of my Helena Heal, my great aunt and only living relative. She was the Dean at Hidden Hall, the university I attended to help guide me in my spiritual gifts.

"Those are good for getting pregnant." The red tips of Aunt Helena's pointy boots were the only thing sticking out from the small funnel cloud.

There was a sudden burst of a black cloak. The tips of red gloved fingers uncurled the long silky coat, exposing my Aunt. Her A-line black dress covered her from throat to the tops of her boots.

Hiss, hiss. Mr. Prince Charming's arm was the only thing outstretched from underneath the table as he batted at the wind.

The tip of the red boots stomped back at his white paws and he withdrew.

"That's what I thought." Aunt Helena tugged the long elbow gloves off of each finger, one at a time in the most dramatic fashion.

I smiled from the inside out that she'd come to see me. Since we didn't live in the same village and it was a bit of a process for me to travel to see her, it was rare that we got to visit.

"I came as soon as I heard the news," she referred to the Whispering Falls Gazette. "What's happening around here?"

"Good to see you too." I put the chalk down and walked over to her, though her observation of the herbs didn't go unnoticed. I ran my fingers through my bangs to get them back in place before I wrapped my arms around her. "The young lady was one of those oil representatives."

"Oil what?" She asked. Aunt Helena was a fierce woman. "Another homeopathic cureist in Whispering Falls?"

"No. Nothing like that." I went back to the chalkboard and picked up the chalk again to finish what was written there. "She was a mortal who sold those . . ."

"Fake oils?" She finished what I was thinking, but didn't want to say.

"Not necessarily fake. I think they were just like Darla's and she did make good money at it, but I'm not so sure why someone killed her." I read what I wrote out loud, "Pregnant? Trying to have a baby?"

"Those words are trying to tell you something." Her brows rose.

"The mix of smells will bring you closure, but not until a few days will be over." I nodded proudly remembering what Madame Torres had told me so early this morning. "This has to be a clue in the murder."

"June, dear," Aunt Helena swept across the shop floor. Her fingers drummed together. "You aren't going to get involved with this Gabby person's death, are you?"

Her words weren't so much phrased as a question, but more as a stern you're not going to.

"I'm going to tell Oscar what I know. Isn't that what a good wife and spiritualist is supposed to do?" I questioned her. "You're the one who taught me everything I know."

"You are very right, but I'm not going to put you in danger or harm." She pushed back her long auburn hair that I so much admired.

"You know that I'm going to be careful," I assured her. "And there are some things I can't forget and ignore or the Order of Elders will be here in the snap of a bat's wing."

"Pffft," she pish-poshed the four old elders that showed up when something went wry in Whispering Falls. "It's a mortal thing, not a spiritual thing."

"It still took place here." I put my foot down. "You've never lived in a village. You've always been in the happy walls of the University."

"Happy? Geesh." Her eyes grew big. "You come and teach for a semester and tell me what you think."

"Teach? Me?" My head tipped back, and great deal of laughter poured out of me. My chin tilted down and when I saw she was stone-cold faced, I shut my lips. "You're joking."

"June Heal," she had that teacher voice, "when have I ever joked? We have an opening in the fall and I think you need to go apply for it. It's all about potions, potion building, and intuition."

I moved around the shop and straightened the displays. My back was to her, which meant she didn't see the smile that'd replaced the laughter.

"Potion building?" I admit that it did sound intriguing. "That's something that sounds fun. Why didn't they have that class when I was there?"

"Who are you talking to?" A woman stood at the door. Her face was blotchy and her eyes were bloodshot.

"I'm sorry." I looked around, but Aunt Helena wasn't there. She was great at disappearing. She had that fantastic spiritual ability to transport and disappear in a jiffy. It was a gift I was envious of. "I thought you were someone else. Are you okay?"

I walked over to the snack table.

"Let me get you a nice warm cup of tea," I suggested as I poured a ladle full in one of the cups. I put one of Wicked Good Bakery sunshine cookies on a paper towel and handed them both to her. "You could use a little pick me up."

"I don't know." She shook her head, but still took them. "A day or so ago, I'd taken it without hesitation because I was eating for two."

The water works turned on and the poor girl sobbed and sobbed. Her shoulders bounced up and down. I took the treats back from her and sat them on the table.

"Come back here with me." I took her by the shoulders and guided her to the small stool that sat at the edge of my counter where my friends would sit and talk to me while I worked. I jerked a tissue from the box and handed it to her. "Here you go. You sit here for a minute. I'll be right back."

"It's our first baby and my husband was so excited. Don't get me wrong," she rambled and I could tell it made her feel better to tell her story. While she talked, I continued to do my job. "My husband is so supportive and we are grieving differently. He encourages me that I can get pregnant again, but now I'm scared."

Immediately, I turned around and ran my finger down the front of the bottles sitting on the shelf on my way behind the partition. Without even looking at the names of the herbs that warmed to my fingertip when I touched them, I grabbed them and disappeared behind the partition.

"A dash Geranium," I read the bottle and pinched a piece, throwing it into the calm cauldron. I picked up the next bottle and tipped it over the cauldron, letting a smidgen of the Fennel and some Carrot Seed fall into the mixture. I realized that the bottles that had lit up contained the ingredients that I'd been smelling and that's what the chalk had written as the special of the day. "A little Palmarosa and Vitex should do it." I put the other ingredients in and circled my hand over the cauldron.

The smoking, swirling potion pulsed ivory and ruby globules. The more I moved my hands, the more the cure rose to the top of the cauldron before it took another turn around the edges before the cauldron flipped off. When it turned off by itself, that's how it told me the homemade cure was finished and ready to be bottled.

"Can you do me a favor and pick out one of the empty bottles next to the chalk board?" I peeked my head around the partition and asked her.

"Sure." She stood up and I noticed her tears were dried. Her face was less blotchy.

I watched as she walked up and down along the shelf. It was such an amazing process to watch. These special bottles knew where they wanted to live and who they wanted to help so when she picked out the teal bottle I knew it had really picked her. There was a light pink butterfly painted on the front with the words *fly* written beneath and a thin dyed rope in teal wound around the neck of the potion bottle.

"That's a beautiful choice," I said when she brought it over to me.

There was a spark between our fingers that gave her a smile.

"I don't know why I came here. But I really like you," she said. I could feel her heart warming through her bottle. "You make me feel like the world isn't ending."

"I'll be right back." I offered her a soft smile before I disappeared to put her potion in her bottle.

With the crystal cork top off, I held the bottle over the cauldron and the potion was magically transferred into the bottle. I took in a deep inhale with my hand gripped around the bottle, sending only love and kindness to the girl as she used this special mix that was only for her. I exhaled and opened my eyes as the warmth left my fingers.

Ahem, I cleared my throat and sprayed the cauldron with cleaner before I took the bottle to the customer.

"Here you go." I handed her the bottle. The price was written on the bottle. It was also something I let the potion pick. "All you need to do with the potio. . ." I corrected myself. "Lotion, is to rub it generously all over your belly and your shoulders."

"Belly and shoulders?" Her brows dipped and she dug in her purse.

The bell over the door dinged, signaling a few more customers. This was going to be a good day. I could feel it.

"That's it. You'll feel better in no time." I assured her and put her money in the cash register. "Let me know how you like it."

"Oh, I will." The tears were long replaced by a smiling face. The young woman would be pregnant in no time and it would be a healthy baby. "Thank you." She turned to leave the shop. "Seriously, best stuff around," she told the customers on her way out and stopped briefly to wave goodbye to me.

Chapter Twelve

My intuition was right. The bell over the door of A Charming Cure didn't stop ringing all day. I had to go to the back room for general stock and added a few quick dashes of specialness to all of them. My poor cauldron was going to need a good cleaning and I was just about out of the special cleanser that I could only get at Wands, Potions, and Beyond. This meant that I was going to have to make a trip to Hidden Hall, A Spiritualist University.

"That's the last of it." I held the bottle to Mr. Prince Charming after I'd sprayed the last of the cleanser in the cauldron and even unscrewed the lid to dump in what little bit couldn't be distributed through the spray mechanism.

He didn't seem to care because he jumped on the seat of the chair behind the counter and curled up into a snuggly ball to take a nap.

The bell over the door dinged.

"June?" Oscar's voice fell across the room and over the partition.

"Back here," I called. "Can you flip the sign and lock the door?" I asked knowing he'd do it.

Quickly I wiped down the cauldron and found Oscar walking back to me. His eyes softened when my eyes caught his. His set jaw relaxed, and a simple closed mouth smile crossed his face.

"What's wrong?" I met him in front of the counter and wrapped my arms around him. Without even dipping into my intuition, I knew there was something wrong.

"You aren't going to like what I've got to do." His breath was warm on my bare neck. Though he sounded down, he made my heart flutter and that was no magic. It was love. I loved Oscar Park since the day he and his uncle had moved in across the street from me and Darla.

"Does this call for a Ding Dong?" It was my way of telling him that no matter what he had to tell me, or what he ever did, there was nothing we couldn't face together.

"Ding Dong. Not a June's Gem?" He asked.

"Adeline gave me a real box." I winked as my hand traveled down his arm to grab his hand. I dragged him around the counter and took out the box of Ding Dongs Adeline had given me as a gift for having her over for supper. "You only have yourself to thank for getting me hooked on these."

I opened the box and he took a couple out, unwrapping one for him and for me.

"Cheers." We clinked our round, chocolaty treats. My teeth broke through the hard outer shell and into the smooth, spongy cake.

Since Darla never let me eat sweets, unless it was my birthday, Oscar's house had been full of plenty. When I was a young girl and on a particular bad day where Darla and I had an argument, Oscar had tapped on my bedroom window and I snuck out with him. We really thought we were rebels, but we only hung out under the tree in his front yard with his box of Ding Dongs.

I wasn't sure if it was Oscar's presence that had made me feel better and I wasn't going to admit to that at the young age. So I told him that it was the Ding Dongs that made me feel better. Through the years, they'd become my go to snack and his too.

Tonight seemed like a perfect time to have one.

"These do make me so happy," I said and gave him a kiss on the lips.

"That makes me so happy." He drew me in and gave me a kiss that sent chills clear down to the tips of my toes.

Rowl! Mr. Prince Charming jumped off the chair and darted away, interrupting our kiss. This was probably his plan the whole time.

"He knows how to ruin a moment," Oscar said.

"Maybe, he knows that you need to tell me what you came in here to tell me." I tried to put the negative into a more positive light because I could feel the heaviness of the situation. "Does this have to do with Gabby?"

"Yeah." He ran his hand through his hair before he brought it down to rest on his police utility belt. "There's enough evidence to name Leah LeRoy as my number one suspect."

My eyes widened with surprise, but he showed no reaction. This told me that he had some really incriminating stuff on her.

"I had to go serve her the village arrest." He looked down and shuffled the toe of his shoe.

He was referring to the by-law that if a spiritualist was accused of a crime, they couldn't run their shop and they couldn't leave the village until the town council voted on the case after the Wizard police of Whispering Falls had presented the evidence before them.

"This is a little more difficult since this involves a mortal. There was a woman who came forward to claim Gabby's body." He frowned. "She's from Locust Grove."

"What's her name? Maybe Adeline knows her." I wondered about Gabby and how she told me that she had no one.

"Beth Phipps. She is actually a friend that'd come to Crazy Crafty Chicks to find out if Gabby had done her Lifestyle oil show there because she never made it back. Both of them sold for the Lifestyle company."

"Can you tell me what evidence you have on Leah?" I asked in hopes he'd share with me because he never liked to mix work with our home life. "I get a feeling you're needing my help."

"You're so good at your gift." He unsnapped the button on his uniform shirt and pulled out his notebook. "What do you know about black locust?"

"Oh the most loveliest of white flowers that dangle down like bells." I remember Darla growing them near the shed. Then I remember Darla say *don't touch those*. "Those are special and if in the wrong hands, the black locust can be deadly," I said what she'd told me out loud.

"June?" Oscar waved his hand in front of me and brought me out the trance I'd suddenly dove into.

"Oscar," I gasped. "Darla used to grow it by the shed. She said they were deadly if gotten in the wrong hands. Is that how Gabby died?"

"Constance Karima told me she was killed by slow death of black locust poisoning." He read off his notes. "It was absorbed into her bloodstream over a period of time."

"Have you let the mortal media know?" I asked.

"No. They obviously don't know the Karima sisters can do an autopsy with a snap of their fingers. They think the autopsy report will come out in a week or so like theirs take." He flipped the notebook shut and stuck it back in his pocket. "That'll keep them away while I get down to the who killed her."

"You said Leah." I was confused.

"From what Beth had told me, Leah owed Gabby a favor. Leah and Gabby had gotten into a fight a few times before Leah caved in and let Gabby come to Whispering Falls to do the presentation. Gabby said that after she did the show at Crafty Crazy Chick, it was going to be the last of her friendship with Leah." His lips pressed together.

"The black locust was in the bottle that rolled out of her hand."

"The bottle that I gave Leah at the smudge ceremony to give back to Gabby?" I asked.

"Yep," he let out a long sigh. "I did some research on the black locust and found that it grows in a small region out west and larger regions east of us in the Virginia areas."

"We don't have villages in the Virginia area so where would Leah get it?" I questioned. Then it hit me like a brick in the gut. "KJ."

"That's right." He nodded. "I went to see him and he said that Leah had bought some black locust seeds from him a couple of months ago before spring."

The Magical Cures Book sparked a bright light from underneath the counter. I rushed around, grabbed it and placing it on top. Oscar and I watched as the pages rapidly flipped and abruptly stopped.

"The seeds of the black locust, if ingested, can kill in five to ten minutes," I read from the book. I glanced up at him. "If crushed and put into something, it would cause blood poisoning, leading to a slow death."

"You talked to Gabby. Did she seem sick to you?" he asked.

"She said she was tired, but my intuition told me she was somewhat depressed, though she told me she was making six figures selling the oils." My memory rolled back and replayed in my head like a movie reel. "The night of the party, I'd gone to the back room of Leah's shop to see why Madame Torres was summoning me. The back door had slammed." Then my mouth opened and all of Gabby's words flew out of my mouth. "You are a crook and I'm not going to let you get away with it. So you're going to have to kill me to keep my mouth shut."

"Did you see who she said that to?" His face lit up as if I had more information to give him.

"No." The word came out in a whisper. "I'm sorry. Whoever she was talking to had slammed the door. By the time Gabby excused herself and I looked out the door, the person was gone."

"Where was Leah during all of this?" He asked a very good question because I clearly remember that she wasn't present during the ordeal.

"I don't know. Gabby had mentioned Leah because Leah had crocheted the little bags the oil bottles came in. Why would Leah go to all the trouble to make all of those if there was something going on between them?" I asked.

"Leah called the Order of Elders as I was questioning her." His nostrils flared with frustration. "Now I have to deal with them."

"Oh, great," I mumbled, knowing that if she called them, all of Whispering Falls was going to be under a microscope. "That means we're going to have to work fast if we are going to try to figure this out before the Marys get here."

The Marys were the Order of Elders. It just so happened all of them were named Mary.

Mary Lynn, Mary Ellen and Mary Sue. All of them were different ages and different in their views spritualty. Luckily for us, they were the elders for all the villages and it would take them a few days to take care of what they were currently working on before they could make it to Whispering Falls.

Chapter Thirteen

Oscar left me with a lot to think about. He went to finish up some paperwork while I cleaned the shop and began to refill the displays with the stock from the back since I was almost wiped out. I wasn't complaining. It'd been a great day of sales and it made me feel so much better about the shop.

In the back of my mind, I knew I needed to get some bottles ready for Adeline at the Piggly Wiggly. My products were in a few mortal stores like the Piggly Wiggly. The bottles were usually bland and boring like the ones Lifetsyle used thanks to how the mortal world worked. It was the magic inside that made my product stand out above the rest. Still, I had to fill the boring bottles and the best time to quickly do so was while the shop was closed. I used the same product with a dash of magic.

I carried the box of empty bottles and placed it on the counter. I used the same ingredients and recipe and tossed all them into the cauldron.

"We are going to have to go to the store quicker than I thought," I said to Mr. Prince Charming when he jumped up on the counter.

Mewl, mewl. Mr. Prince Charming looked at the front door of the shop.

"What is it?" I asked him and left the cauldron simmering, peeking my head around the partition.

Leah was standing at the door, waving as though she were trying to get my attention.

I hurried around the counter and unlocked the door.

"Get in here." Immediately I drew her into my arms. "Leah, what's going on?" I let her go and reached over to lock the door back.

"I know you know that I'm the number one suspect who killed Gabby, but I didn't do it." Her brows dipped as the tears poured out of her eyes. "I don't know how the seeds got into that bottle. But someone wanted her dead and framed me."

"But you did buy the black locust from KJ?" I asked, knowing that I was going to have to go see KJ myself. I didn't know much about the poisonous plant but I needed to. My gut told me so.

"Yes. I did. I was going to plant some at my house. After I left his shop, I had a line waiting for me outside of Crazy Crafty Chick. Once I got everyone inside, I put the seeds down and forgot all about them." She was shaking like a leaf.

"Here." I poured her some tea from the snack table and gave her some cookies. "Go back there and sit while I clean this up for the night. You need to drink something to calm down so we can talk through this."

There was no sense in talking to her when she was this upset. She wouldn't be in her right mind to formulate the answers that I needed to get down to the bottom of all of this in her current state.

If what she said about how she put the seeds down was true, anyone could've gotten them. But, this would've been back in the spring. Had she been associating with Gabby that long? If that was the case, this was a premeditated murder.

Leah did what I told her to do. Mr. Prince Charming had even found a comfortable spot on her lap and had curled up in a ball with his eyes shut tight. This told me that she wasn't a killer and her greatest fear that someone had set her up, was right. But who would either not like Leah or not care enough about Leah to pin a murder on her?

"Do you remember anything from that day that stood out to you?" I asked and put the complimentary cookies for the customers away so they wouldn't get stale overnight. She shook her head. "I'm not trying to read you, but sometimes when I feel danger, or something is off, my gift gives me a little nudge or sign. Do you recall your yarn talking to you that day?"

The heavy lashes that shadowed her cheeks flew up.

"Yes!" she yelled.

Mr. Prince Charming jumped up and down, scurrying back to the comforts underneath a display table.

She stood up.

"I had a light pink cashmere yarn that'd just come in. I was unpacking it that afternoon." Her eyes darted back and forth, and her voice was escalating as she remembered more and more. "It was perfect for a baby blanket. When I saw it I was so happy, but then I touched it and such sadness came over me." She fell to her knees.

"Leah, are you okay?" I bent down next to her.

"Yes. It's a heavy sadness. A death." She buried her head in her hands. "My heart is breaking for a baby."

"Do still have it?" I asked.

"No." she looked up at me with the clearest of eyes. "A man came in and bought it."

"Was he from our mortal neighborhood?" I asked for any lead she could remember.

"No." She shook her head. "But now I know."

"Know what?" I questioned her.

"Gabby Summerfield was pregnant." She faltered like a wilting flower.

The chalkboard lit up in a bright pink light. Geranium, Fennel, Carrot Seed, Palmarosa, and Vitex glowed in black.

"That's what Madame Torres meant," I gasped and looked at Leah with wide-awake eyes. I didn't tell her about the forecast Madame Torres had told me because if there was any chance that I could help Leah, I had to use my gift for the investigation and not let it out into the village in case the real killer was listening. "Is there anyone who you think would want to pin this on you?"

"No," she said in a stern voice. "Does this mean you're going to help me?"

"Oscar told me that you called in the Order of Elders and their investigations take forever from what I recall from the past," I told her since she was fairly new to the village and probably not been involved too much with the Marys.

"My parents told me when I left Alabama to immediately call in the Marys if I ever got in trouble." Her chest started to heave up and down as though she was going to start crying all over again.

"Don't cry. You've got to be strong and think about this. Think back to that guy who bought the baby yarn." I had a gut feeling that this guy either knew Gabby or knew something about her. "Have you ever had any men come into your store to buy yarn?"

Not that I was discriminating against men who crocheted, but more times than not, it was the women who came in to get the yarn.

"He asked all sorts of questions and read from a piece of paper on the exact yarn type. Cashmere." She was starting to remember some fact, which were good.

"Do you remember what he looked like? How old he was? Tall? Short?" I wanted to get as many details as possible because when I tracked down Gabby's co-worker, Beth, I was planning on asking if she knew Gabby was pregnant.

"He was average build. Probably as tall as Oscar, if that helps." Deep-set worry was in her eyes. She jumped to her feet. "He had a very blonde eyebrow on the right." She tapped her eyebrow as she began to recall more and more. "I thought it was odd because his hair was brown and his left brow was also brown."

"That could be a distinct birthmark, so that's good." I nodded in hopes that this one light browed guy had lived in Locust Grove and maybe Adeline had seen him. She was good at recognizing people who came into her grocery store and obviously this guy would stand out.

"Other than that, I gave him the yarn and haven't seen him or those seeds since." Her bottom lip curled between her teeth as she chewed on it. She began to shake her head. "I can't remember anything else."

"When I was at your shop for the Lifestyle oil presentation, I was checking on something in private and I walked into you back room by the backdoor before Gabby started and she was having a heated discussion with someone." I knew that I wasn't allowed to read other spiritualists, but this was only to help her. So I gave myself permission and would suffer the consequences later. I zeroed in on her body language to get a good reading.

"Whoever she was talking to had hurried out your shop's back door, slamming it."

"Really?" She asked, blinking with bafflement.

Nothing about her response told me she was covering anything up.

"Unfortunately, I didn't see who it was. Where were you during the presentation? I noticed you were gone," I said.

"You don't think I had a fight with her and left my own shop, do you?" As casually as she could manage, she added. "I was at Wicked Good Bakery picking up the goodies I'd gotten for the customers who'd come so they could shop Gabby's product and enjoy some treats. No different than you do."

"I'm not accusing you of anything. If you want me to help you, then I have to know everything you did from the time you got up the day you bought those seeds until this morning." It wasn't going to be easy, but I knew in my intuition that she didn't kill Gabby. "Why did you owe Gabby a favor?"

"Oh my gosh." She sounded so desperate. "Oh my gosh." She started to pace back and forth in front of the counter. "How did you know?" She wrung her hands together.

"Calm down," I urged her in a calm voice. "You have to tell me everything."

Now her reaction sent my intuition into overtime. There was something wrong and I was now going to second guess myself. That was never a good thing. The first thing in intuition school was to never second-guess your gift.

"How did you know?" She asked again through gritted teeth and a wall of tears.

"A co-worker of Gabby's came to the police station and wanted to file a missing person's report with Oscar," I told her. "She told Oscar that Gabby was here after you owed her a favor, but she never named the favor. She also said that you and Gabby didn't really get along, making it seem that Gabby had something against you that would make you want her gone. Not in a good way either."

"June, I'm a simple spiritualist from the south. I don't want to bring harm to no one. I just want to play with my yarn and be happy." She talked so fast that it made her appear desperate and that didn't sit well with my gut. "I didn't know Gabby before I moved here. She was one of my first customers. She would buy yarn and then bring it back. She'd complain how it wouldn't fit her needles properly or how she didn't like the stitches once she made them. I never said anything to her but once." Her mood veered sharply to anger. Her jaw tensed, her nose flared and her breath became labored. "The last time she came into the shop as a customer, it was just the two of us. She was complaining and when I took the yarn from her, I accidently cast a spell. It was from a dark and evil place in my soul. She felt the shift and it knocked her on the ground."

"Leah," I sighed and looked out the window, noticing a woman had parked in front of the police station and gone inside. "We are never to let the mortal world see our gifts. We have an oath to keep our gifts to the village and use them for good," I said, putting my head back into the present moment.

It was no excuse for her to use the spell, but it was worse that she used the spell directly in front of Gabby.

"I covered it up by telling her I was sorry I knocked her down, but I was tired of her coming to my shop and returning perfectly good quality yarn. You know I don't sell bad quality anything." She shifted her focus on trying to get me to believe she was a good shop owner instead of hitting the root of the issue. Gabby. "Then she told me that I'd done some sort of crazy voodoo something on her and she saw it and felt it. I told her that no one would believe her."

"You need to focus on Gabby and what happened after you tried to get her to forgive you." I said in a controlled tone, "What did she say to you after she got up?"

"She told me that she didn't care if no one believed her that she'd sue me for hitting her. She rubbed her arm and leg saying that I hurt her. It was like she flipped on a dime." Leah sniffed. "That's when she told me I had to host a Lifestyle party for her at my shop and and then she'd drop the charges."

"How long ago was this argument?" I asked wondering how close to the purchase of the black locust seed was to the incident. She looked at me a little confused. "Had you already bought the seeds at this time?"

"No. I bought them that afternoon." Her words didn't make me feel any better. "What is that look on your face?"

"If you'd bought the seeds previous to this, then I know you wouldn't get a premeditated charge meaning first degree murder." I thought aloud. "It clearly looks like she was holding this party over your head. You then bought

the seeds and planned to poison her the day of the party." I
let the ideas roll from my head and out my mouth.

"If that was the case, I'd have killed her that week so I
didn't have to go through the process of hosting the party. I
fought with her for those couple of months trying to see if
she'd forget or decide not to have it. I told her that you
were here, and the village didn't like other vendors coming
in. Then she went and got the fake rules we post for the
mortals and she didn't see any rules against her coming to
the shop." Leah continued to tell me how the party
developed over the past few months. "Every week, she'd
call and ask me when I was going to host the party. A week
ago, her lawyer came in and handed me a piece of paper
that said if I didn't have the party as we agreed, then they
were going to file the complaint."

"Do you have those papers?" I asked.

"I do." She nodded with a little more hope in her tone.

"Does it have the lawyer's name on it?" I asked.

"I'm sure it does." She managed to reply with a stiff
lip. "Why?"

"I want it and I want to go see them. If we can
establish that she was blackmailing you, maybe she was
blackmailing someone else." I shrugged not fully knowing

where I was going with it, but I was going somewhere. "Finding this guy with the blonde brow might help us too."

"How are you going to do that?" she asked.

"You asked me to help you, right?" I asked and got confirmation. "Then you do what Oscar told you to do and leave this all up to me. Where are those papers from Gabby's lawyer?"

"In my shop," she said.

"Can you get them?" I asked knowing it was going to be going against the ruling Oscar had given her via the by-laws.

"Yes. It might be a day or two since I'm not allowed to go in there, but I can get them." She was confident and I liked that.

"You bring them to me when you have them. Understood?" I questioned.

"Understood." She turned and walked to the door. She unlocked it and twisted the handle. "Thank you, June," she said over her shoulder before she walked out.

"Don't thank me yet." I pulled back the curtain in the front window and watched her disappear into the dusk of the night. A coldness poured over me.

Chapter Fourteen

While I was getting prepared to work on the bottles for the Piggly Wiggly, there was a tap on the door. When I looked to see who it was, I realized it was the same woman who'd parked in front of the police station while I had been talking to Leah.

"Good evening," she greeted me with a smile. "I'm Nina Teeter from Lifestyle and I've got one of your bottles from Gabby Summerfield that was on order." She held up the bag.

"Please," I opened the door wide, "come in. I'd completely forgotten about that bottle."

"I'm trying to get myself together, so I can deliver the products her customers had placed without skipping a beat. It'd be what she wanted." She sighed and looked around the shop. "She told me about you and your shop. She said you were a fascinating woman."

"You talked to her?" I questioned.

"Of course. She called me after the show at Crafty Crazy Chick to report her numbers. I'm the regional consultant." She walked around the shop and picked up a couple of bottles.

Her body left me feeling sad and lonely, longing for Darla. It was when I began to tap into my intuition that I realized this woman wasn't here by accident. She needed a potion for depression. The depression wasn't for a loved one, it was for her life and how she'd been living her life.

"Tell me about the business." I encouraged her to talk because the more she revealed, the more I could understand her hurt and what she needed, not to mention she might uncover something that had to do with Gabby's murder.

"I started selling Lifestyle about five years ago when the oils started to become popular. At the time I lived in California and you know they like anything out there." She offered a nice warm smile. "I moved to Locust Grove because the cost of living is cheaper, and no one was selling Lifestyle at the moment and if I wanted to move up in the company, I knew I was going to have to be a regional. They wanted to expand, and I took it." She uncorked a bottle to smell it. "Gabby had such a bright future."

"I take it that you were close?" I could feel the sorrow.

"I loved her like a daughter. I don't have a daughter. She was so eager to learn. I spent a lot of time with her. Then she brought her friend, Beth, on board. She's good but not like Gabby was good. Certainly, not like a daughter either." There was a sarcastic, yet gentle, tone to her voice.

"Whispering Falls is so small, that I did notice you earlier when you went into the police station," I said and watched as she circled the shop.

"Yes. Gabby doesn't have any family and I really wanted to make sure the police here weren't only on top of the investigation, but I also wanted to claim her body so I can give her a proper funeral." Her eyes filled with tears and it broke my heart.

I walked over to her and put my arm around her shoulder to give her a hug, but really dive into my intuition to see what I could concoct to make her feel better, not that I could take away the painful loss of Gabby. I pulled away and began to walk towards the counter.

"I think I have just the thing for you. Not that you don't need another lotion, but this one is on me." I winked and disappeared behind the partition.

The jade liquid in the cauldron was at a rolling boil. I plucked off a leaf of the Passion Flower and tossed it into the potion. A puff of smoke exploded above the pot in a dust of white powder that smelled like baby powder. My heart sank knowing that Nina had loved Gabby as her own daughter. The smell of the lotion would take on the scent of baby powder but seep into her soul to help heal her wounded heart. I threw in an eyelash of toad, moving the liquid into a pulsing round motion that changed colored to pale pink, a perfect shade for Gabby's memory.

Once the cauldron shut off, I walked back around the partition and found Nina standing in front of the empty bottles.

"I wish Lifestyle came in beautiful bottles like these." She turned around and had a cobalt blue bottle in her hand.

"Here, let me fill that for you." I reached out and took the bottle from her. "On the house."

I hurried back to the cauldron and held the bottle over the top to let the magic do its thing. When it was finished, I went back into the shop and handed her the filled bottle.

"I made this for you. Just rub it on your chest twice a day." The smell would help her ease up on herself and the potion would enter her skin immediately to help heal her heart.

She smiled and popped off the cork lid. She held it underneath her nose and smelled it.

"It smells like baby powder." Her eyes slide up to me with tears hanging on the edge of her eyelids. "I used to tell Gabby that I was going to start putting baby powder on her because I'd always dreamed of having a baby girl to lather in the smell good lotion."

"I'm so sorry. From when I talked with her, she was a very sincere and sweet girl." I knew my words weren't much comfort, but the little spell inside of the bottle would do her wonders.

"Thank you," She held the bottle to her heart. "You know, if you ever want to sell Lifestyle, I think you'd be perfect." She dropped one hand and put it in the outside pocket of her purse, pulling out a card and held it out to me.

"I think I've got my hands full here," I said but took her business card anyways.

"Well, if something changes." She held the bottle up in a cheers sort of way. "Thank you," she called on her way out the door.

Chapter Fifteen

Oscar had called the shop while I was finishing up the bottles for the Piggly Wiggly. He was going to be working late so he told me to head on home without him.

The sky had turned into a nice purple as the dusk blanketed the village. It was much too pretty to even think about going home and sitting alone. I'd told Eloise that I'd check on her and wanted to keep my word.

I sent Mr. Prince Charming ahead of me to let her know I was on my way. The fond memories of finding out exactly how Eloise was a part of my life before I knew it made me feel so much better since I'd been thinking about Leah the entire night.

Eloise had befriended Darla and they were best friends. Since my dad had married Darla, everyone knew that Darla was in on their little village secrets. Eloise didn't hide her potions or her gift from Darla, which she should've but she lived outside of the village since. She was considered a bad-sider at the time, even though she was the most kind-hearted spiritualist I knew.

Anyways, Darla wrote about Eloise in the Magical Cures Book. She talked about how their friendship developed and how funny Eloise was. She even helped Darla make a few fun twists to Darla's cures. Eloise was there when I was born and she even babysat me when Darla was at A Dose of Darla.

Even though I didn't remember Eloise, the same way Oscar hadn't known his past, with the journal entries in the book, I felt like I knew her. When I went to her house, I could feel the enchantment that Darla had written about.

Darla was able to describe the trail going around the gathering rock and walking deep into the woods. As I took that same walk, the fog was beginning to roll in but it didn't stop me from smiling when between a couple of trees, I could see Eloise's two-story house that was built on a platform, high off the ground. There was a set of wooden stairs that led up to a cozy wrap-around porch.

I didn't bother going up them, because the gas-lit lanterns that dotted the cobblestone walkway to her private garden were glowing, lighting the way.

The darkness of the night that was on me disappeared into a colorful display of beautiful and vibrant purple, green, red, orange, and yellow flowers that she'd planted on each side of the walk.

My heart raced every time I walked into her garden. It was a dream to have the neat rows of herbs skillfully planted and proportioned perfectly. Each row had a painted wood sign with the names of the herbs like rose petals, moonflower, mandrake root, seaweed, shrinking violet, dream dust, fairy dust, magic peanut, lucky clover, steal rose, spooky shroom. All the ingredients I loved to use in my potions.

Mr. Prince Charming's tail waved me over to the gazebo.

"June, You're here right on time." Eloise stood under the gazebo, neatly arranging an assortment of candy on tiered displays and containers.

"Are we having a sugar party?" I questioned with laughter.

"I've been thinking a lot since I found Gabby Summerfield's body this morning." She drummed her fingers together. "I know she wasn't there the first-time I cleansed of the village. She'd been dead a while, so someone must've seen me and waited to drag her out. They wanted her to be found." She made a good point.

"If they wanted her to be found, then maybe they did care about her and it wasn't some willy-nilly killing." I continued with her thought.

"I definitely think she was murdered on purpose." Eloise looked out into the garden as though she were pondering more. "I'm just not sure why she was murdered. That is why I'm hosting a little get-together for the teenagers. They knew something was up and came to get me. I didn't catch on to what they were lightening up about at the time, so they might be able to tell me now."

"I wonder if we should have Petunia come to the candy party," I suggested.

"Great idea. She can communicate with them." Eloise pointed to Mr. Prince Charming, then used her fingernail to slowly scratch underneath his chin. He purred. His tail swayed in time with her fingernail. His lips curled up. His eyes were narrow. "Would you be a dear and go fetch Petunia?"

She pulled her finger away and he didn't hesitate before he darted out of the garden. Eloise sat down in one of the café table chairs.

"He's a sucker for a good scratch." I joked. "She was pregnant," I blurted out.

"Who? Gabby?" Her brows rose. With a tip of her head, she motioned me to the chair next to her.

"Yes. Her friend came to see Oscar at the station when Gabby hadn't returned to Locust Grove. She also told him that Gabby and Leah had a fight. When I asked Leah about it, Gabby had been blackmailing her to have a party because she walked in on Leah just as Leah was casting." I cringed thinking of Eloise's reaction. "Gabby had returned something to Leah and Gabby felt the spell, knocking her down. Leah tried to tell Gabby that she hit her, but Gabby said that she felt some sort of voodoo Leah put on her and was using that to blackmail her."

Just as I imagined. The fog lifted as her mood soured. There was a red cloud that formed over us when Eloise stood up. She walked down the few steps of the gazebo and stopped in the middle of her garden with her arms outstretched.

"What is the friend's name?" Her voice boomed like thunder.

"Beth," I said loud enough for her to hear without my voice cracking. Even though I knew Eloise held a lot of power, I'd never seen her go into a mad, almost angry state.

The red cloud floated down just enough for Eloise's outstretched fingertips to touch the edges. The lightning bolts darted around her, barely missing her body.

"Beth and her actions against the village of Whispering Falls. I hereby freeze Beth and bind her from causing harm to our community. As my will so mote it be," Eloise repeated this over and over.

The words appeared in form and crawled up the lightning bolts, drawing up into the red cloud.

With each word and penetration of the lightening, the cloud got smaller and smaller as if it were soaking up the spell Eloise was putting on Beth until the cloud was no more.

Slowly, she brought her arms down to her side and brushed her hands together.

"That should do it until we can look further into this mess." She walked over. Her eyes drew past the gazebo. "Welcome sweet teenagers."

The glow of thousands of lightning bugs swarmed the garden as they flittered about. Each one of them blinking at different times, creating the most beautiful glow over the very spot that was just in upheaval. I got up to let them have the candy stations.

"Come, come." She waved them over. "Eat and enjoy."

We stood there as the candy began to disappear. It was so funny how such little beings could eat candy so fast, but what teen didn't like candy? Eloise had something for everyone.

"What did you just do to Beth?" I had to ask. She sucked in a deep breath as if she were contemplating whether or not to tell me. "I only ask because Leah asked me to help her. I know she didn't do it. And I know I broke the by-law, and Oscar is going to be frustrated with me, but I can't let her go to jail if she didn't do it."

"I wanted to make sure to stop Beth's memory if she knew something about why Gabby and Leah were fighting or whatever it is that Gabby had told her. It will give us time to figure out what happened to Gabby," she said.

"Black locust seeds killed her."

"Wonderful. Then we can go see KJ to see who bought them." She shrugged with an upbeat tone.

"Leah LeRoy bought them," I hated to say.

Eloise jerked around and looked at me stunned.

I quickly told her what I knew about the seeds that'd disappeared the same day the man came into the Crafty Crazy Chick with a piece of paper to get a certain yarn.

"Leah said the yarn was sad?" Eloise's chin lifted in the air. Her eyes narrowed. "Very interesting. And Gabby was pregnant?"

"Yes." Both of us looked at the front of the garden when we hard footsteps.

"Did you summon me?" Petunia walked into the glow of the lightning bugs light with a net over her hair and a sleepy look on her face. "This better be good, because Gerald gets all upset like Orin if Orin wakes up and wants me. Then I have to attend to two babies."

"June had a wonderful idea and I'd like to try it." Eloise swept up to her while Mr. Prince Charming dashed over to the gazebo to scare the teens.

"Stop that," I warned him before he could put his plan into action.

Like a scardey-cat, all four clawed paws dug into the earth to stop him, jerking him into a different direction and he speed off into the night.

"What idea was that, June?" Petunia had a peeked interest.

"The teenagers came to get Eloise the night of Gabby's death, only Eloise didn't know what they wanted." I continued to tell her how Eloise followed them, but nothing was there so she began her cleansing ceremony. "We think they saw something. Since you can communicate with them, we thought you might ask them to tell us what they saw."

"You do not believe Leah LeRoy did it?" she questioned. "As the village President I must consider these things before I even attempt to get into the middle of things. As a matter of fact, I'm hesitant because Officer Park told me she summoned the Marys."

"She what?" Eloise gasped, drawing her cape around her and across her face.

"She's young. She was only doing what her parents told her to do and I think we have time before the Marys get here to figure this out. I told her I'd help her." I knew that I had to tell Petunia and this came with the consequences that Oscar was going to find out.

"I find that a suitable argument." She smiled.

"Thank you." I hugged her. "I'm positive Leah didn't kill Gabby."

"Positive as in reading her positive?" She looked at me with scolding eyes.

"Because she came to me for help." I didn't deny or accept her claim. I simply state the truth, just leaving a few parts out.

It must've been enough of an answer to satisfy her because she left Eloise and I standing there while she walked over to the teens.

We watched as she gestured with her hands and they gathered around her, putting a spotlight on her. Her head moved in rapid movement and spoke in a low buzz that I didn't understand. With the different sequences of lights from their bodies, they seemed to be talking back to her. She nodded and turned around.

"You'll find something near the border between Locust Grove and Whispering Falls. They didn't see any particulars, just the floating down of the object. Only the object in mention was originally at the Crazy Crafty Chick shop before they came to get Eloise." Petunia didn't bother with any more information. She walked out of the garden.

Chapter Sixteen

It was too late to go to the border without someone seeing me. Even though Petunia, Eloise and Oscar knew I was going to try and help Leah, I couldn't risk the other spiritualist finding out. It was the big no-no that would get the Marys here quicker than we needed them to be.

Oscar had sent me a text saying he was still at the office was going to try and get some shut-eye there. It was his way of telling me that he wasn't coming home for the night.

The next morning before any shops opened, Mr. Prince Charming and I drove the Green Machine down the hill and parked in front of A Charming Cure. He didn't budge from his favorite curled up position on the dashboard. He knew where he found the warmth of the heater blowing on him, shielding him from the bit of chill in the air would soon be long gone.

I loaded up the boxes for Adeline at the Piggly Wiggly. It was a perfect cover up to check out the border and what the teenagers said I'd find there.

"Welcome to Whispering Falls, A Charming Village," reading the old wood sign to welcome tourists still made a smile cross my lips. We did live in a charming community where everyone looked out for each other.

I pulled the Green Machine to the side of the road.

"I guess you're not moving?" I put the gearshift in park.

Mr. Prince Charming purred with happiness but didn't even open his eyes. It was his favorite spot to lie. Even before we moved to Whispering Falls, I'd find him in the El Camino basking in the sunny spot.

I got out of the car and where the spring had started to turn to summer, the thick vines were covered with the brightest thick, green leaves. As soon as I'd take a step, my shoe would disappear into the depths of the lushness.

"Where are you?" I questioned the item the teens were talking about. "Too bad I don't have a gift for seeking out items."

"June, here!" I heard Eloise call out to me. I hurried towards her voice that was about twenty feet deep behind the wooded area beyond the sign.

"What are you doing here?" I asked.

"You didn't think I wasn't curious, did you?" She questioned with sparkling eyes. "Did you say cashmere pink yarn?"

"Yes." My eyes followed the line of her arm as she extended her thin finger to a heap of pink lying just under the surface of the vines. "Eloise," I gasped when I noticed the piece of the blanket sticking out.

I bent down and noticed the yarn that was used to make the blanket appeared to be the yarn that Leah LeRoy said the man had purchased. My intuition did double time when I touched the edge of the blanket.

"It is the yarn." I drew my hand back and looked up at Eloise. "I have to tell Oscar about it and he needs to come get it to get fingerprints off of it."

"What do you think this has to do with Leah and Gabby?" Eloise asked. "What did the teens see?"

"I think that whoever that man was that came into Leah's shop, knew that Gabby was blackmailing her and that somehow knew about the black locust." I shook my head. "I know none of it makes sense right now, but somehow."

"You have an amazing intuition and I know you're going to figure it out." Eloise put a hand on my shoulder.

"That's why you need to check on the teaching position at Hidden Hall."

"You know about that?" I asked and wondered how. It was my next stop after I went to Locust Grove.

"Helena stopped by. She told me about it since I'm teaching next semester." Eloise had taught there many times. "She thought that if you knew I was going to be there, then you'd be open to thinking about it."

"But if I go, I'd have to stay there all the time and not see Oscar as much. What about my shop?" I asked.

"Faith Mortimer ran your shop when you went to school there. She did a fine job. Plus, you still came home a lot and made your potions." She reminded me that I did have free time to come and go as I pleased as a student and still got my work and my studies completed. "What did Oscar say?"

"I didn't tell him." I stood up and dragged my phone out of my pocket.

"June, you need to." Eloise didn't tell me anything that I didn't already know and I knew would be a hard life change if I did take the job. "You are a teacher by nature. This is part of your job as a spiritualist to grow."

"I know, but we've only been married a year and we've already been through so much." I thumbed through the contacts and stopped when I got to the O's. "Every time we turn around, he's got a murder or I've got a business deal and I was just hoping things would settle down for at least a year so we could. . ." I smiled. "I don't know." I shrugged. "Start a family."

"June!" Eloise clasped her hand over her mouth. "Are you pregnant?"

"Oh, no." I shook my head. "Not at all, but we do want to have children and if we keep doing things for others all the time and not taking time for ourselves, we'll never have the family we want."

"I have a feeling that you need to teach at least one semester before you settle down." She didn't tell me what I wanted to hear, but I admired her for her tenacity. "But that's up to you. I'm just asking that you talk to him about it. Maybe he will have some insight."

"I'm not going to lie, but I did get a tiny bit excited when Aunt Helena mentioned it." I bit back the grin, but it didn't work.

"Look at your face." Her jaw dropped. "You're glowing."

"We'll see." I quickly text Oscar that I'd gotten a lead on the case and there was a pink baby blanket in the vines about twenty feet beyond the Whispering Falls welcome sign. I also told him I'd fill him in after I'd gotten back from Wands, Potions and Beyond.

Eloise and I said our goodbyes, but not without me promising that I'd talk to Oscar this afternoon after got some information from Aunt Helena during my visit to the university to get the cauldron cleaner.

The cell phone rang from deep inside of my bag just as I was about to put the Green Machine in gear.

"Good morning." The sound of Oscar's voice sent my heart soaring. "I missed you last night."

"I missed you too." I sighed. "I'm guessing you got my text."

"I did. Do you think you could bring it by this morning before you run into Locust Grove?" He asked. "Beth is going to come by this morning and give an official statement. I was wondering if you'd like to come and maybe throw out some questions for her?"

"Really?" I ignored Mr. Prince Charming. He was growling and trying to get my attention by batting at the bracelet. "You're asking me to officially help?" I couldn't believe my ears.

It was really a no-brainer for me and something I'd been wanting to do since the day he was sworn in as a cop. I reached behind my seat and grabbed the emergency kit. It had everything you'd possibly need for a roadside emergency and that included garbage bags.

"Yes. I'd like you to use your intuition to talk to her," he said. "And maybe pick up something to eat from Gerald. I'm starving."

I got out of the car and trekked back over to the blanket, carefully picking it up with the bag and letting it fall in so I didn't put any more fingerprints on it. I hurried back to the car.

"I'd love to. I was going to see if Adeline had ever seen this guy with the white brow to help tie him in, but it can wait." I jerked the wheel and pushed the gas, heading straight back into Whispering Falls.

"What guy with the white brow?" Oscar asked.

"Oh. I haven't talked to you about me talking to Leah. I'll explain over breakfast," I said and we hung up the phone. "And I need to talk to you over breakfast about the teaching position," I muttered to myself.

Truly, the only thing that'd keep me from it would be the time I'd have to be away from him.

"What do you think about me taking the teaching position at Hidden Hall?" I asked Mr. Prince Charming, who was now pouting and hiding on the floor board underneath the seat.

"It would mean that we'd be spending a lot less time in Whispering Falls for a few months." I continued to talk to Mr. Prince Charming like he was going to pop up and just start talking. "And a lot less time with Oscar."

That got his attention. He popped his head up from under the seat and looked at me.

"We'd get to see some of the old students and some of the staff." It would be nice to see them on a regular basis. "You'd trade seeing Oscar for Aunt Helena every day."

Rowl. He batted the air with his front paw. He clawed his way out and jumped up on the seat, bringing his paw up to his mouth to clean.

Whispering Falls was starting to wake up. Clouds of yellow dust drifted under the fog, giving it a good lift out of the village. The morning dew that was scuttled over the shop rooftops were glistening as they began to melt away from the peek-a-boo of the promise of the sun's rays.

I pulled the Green Machine in front of Crafty Crazy Chicks and ran across the street into The Gathering Grove with Mr. Prince Charming on my heels. Only once across the street, he darted the other way. No doubt he was going to see Petunia at Glorybee because it was about the time she fed the animals in her shop.

Faith Mortimer was hunched over the trunk of the Wicked Good Bakery delivery car.

"Good morning, Faith," I greeted her. "Are you on your way to Locust Grove?"

"I sure am." She stood up and opened one of the donut boxes she was going to deliver to the Piggly Wiggly, something they did every morning. "Want one?"

"No thanks. But I do have a favor. Do you think you could drop off the lotions to Adeline while you are there?" I asked.

"You know I don't mind. Go grab them." She pointed to the car. "I've got plenty of room in the back seat."

"You are a life saver." I gave her a quick hug and ran back to the Green Machine to get the box. "Thank you so much," I said after I got the box in her car.

The early morning was fading away fast and I still didn't feel like I'd helped Leah in any way. It was so sad to look across the street from the inside of the Gathering Grove and seeing her shop with a *temporarily closed* sign on her door.

"What can I get you this fine morning?" Gerald twirled the right side of his handlebar mustache in his finger and thumb. "What if I get you a nice soufflé?"

"I'll take three. One for me, Oscar and Colton." I narrowed my eyes trying to tell Gerald not to even think about asking me any questions on why I'd summoned his wife to Eloise's last night. "Along with three large coffees, to go." I threw in just so he wouldn't be tempted to put it in a mug and think he was going to get a chance to read my coffee grounds.

Behind me was a young woman with curly red hair that draped over her shoulders.

"What's good here?" She asked in a small voice. The freckles that dotted her face made her look like she had a natural tan.

My intuition told me immediately that she wasn't from here.

"Everything. I'm getting a soufflé this morning and a coffee." I smiled at the stranger.

"I'm a little nervous and coffee probably wouldn't help." She gnawed on the corner of her lip and looked up at the menu behind the counter.

"Why are you nervous?" I asked.

"I know you are a stranger, but I feel drawn to you." She answered as her brows frowned.

"I have that effect on people." I wondered what was going on this her. "If you want, you can come see me at my shop." I pointed out the window. "A Charming Cure and I've got some really good remedies that could help you with whatever ails you."

"No wonder." She clapped her hands together. "I saw your shop yesterday when I was on my way to the police department. I sell Lifestyle oils and I couldn't help but notice your shop."

Like a jolt of caffeine had been injected into my intuition, I knew this was Beth.

"Gerald," I called over the counter. "Make that four soufflés and four coffees."

Chapter Seventeen

After I explained to Beth that I was going to the police station and knew she was going there, we decided to walk down together with the food in the to-go bags. I'd get my car later, after work.

"Gabby was so excited about you giving her information to your friend at the Piggly Wiggly," she said as we walked down towards the police station.

"As a matter of fact, I was going to tell my friend about what happened to Gabby when I dropped off my line of products that sells there, but my friend was going into town this morning and she's taking them for me." It was small talk until we got to the station.

"Hi there." Oscar's face light up when I walked into the door. His eyes were tired, but still the blue was as bright as the Caribbean Sea. "Good morning." His eyes drew past my shoulder and noticed Beth.

"I met Beth while we were in line at The Gathering Grove." I held up the bag. "I got everyone something to eat." I always believed food brought people together in comfort and Beth needed some comfort. "Where's Colton?" I asked.

"He and Amelia went on their annual vacation to visit family last night after he impounded Gabby's car for me." He used vacation as a code word for their visits to other spiritual villages since neither of them were from Whispering Falls or even Kentucky.

"I was wondering why I've not seen Amelia." I said and opened the bag. She was a very good friend of mine and she'd not stopped in the shop, nor was she at the smudge ceremony. "Then we've got plenty to eat." I took out the soufflés and put them on Colton's desk as a table for all of us. I gestured to the food. "Dig in."

"This is a bit unusual." Beth walked over and eased down into one of the chairs in front of the desk. I took the other one and Oscar sat on the edge of the desk.

"If you can't tell, Whispering Falls is a little unusual." My eyes softened as I tried to make her feel more at ease.

The way I figured, was that if we treated her with kindness, she'd open up more than we needed her to. I had to figure out exactly who Gabby was and her blackmail side because she definitely didn't portray that to me when I talked with her.

Oscar gave me the unspoken look where he was going to disappear, and I was going to "friend" Beth.

"You sell Lifestyle like Gabby Summerfield." I dragged my bag from across my body and dug down deep for the roll-on oil. "Gabby sold this to me a couple of days ago." I held the bottle up. "She said it was good for breathing."

"She was so good at what she did. She was top sales person the last few months," Beth said.

I laughed.

"She was good at it. As you know, I own a similar shop." It killed me to even compare the two. "She sold me over five-hundred dollars worth of product." I left out the part that I was going to dissect them to see what the company used to make their false claims.

Beth laughed and took more bites of her food. Her shoulders started to melt down and her eyes began to relax.

"Oscar said you were her best friend." I reached over and touched her hand. "I'm so sorry."

"Did he tell you about her fight with that Leah woman?" She asked as she bent her head to the side to see if Oscar was on his way back up from where he'd disappeared.

"No." I shook my head, lying. "I was at the party. It was a great turnout."

"Gabby tried to tell me that she and this Leah were friends, but they weren't. I caught Gabby on the phone with her and in a deep argument." She brought the cup of coffee up to her lips. While she was drinking, I knew I could throw in a question or two.

"What did they say to each other?" I asked.

"I don't know what Leah said to Gabby because they were on the phone, but I know that Gabby kept telling her that the product was good and she didn't need to make any changes to the plan or the party because it was what was promised to her," she said.

"If you didn't hear Leah, then how do you know it was her?" I asked.

"Gabby told me." She shrugged. "We told each other everything."

"What did she say about Leah?" I asked. "Because I'm just shocked. I mean when Oscar told me that he'd arrested her, I'd never thought that about her. It just goes to show that you really don't know someone when you think they do."

"I knew that Leah owed Gabby a favor. Gabby had given Leah some business by letting her make those crochet bags that looks like something my great-grandmother would make. I told Gabby they were ugly. She laughed and assured me that it was only to get to her foot in the door of Whispering Falls." She took another drink. I let the silence hang between us because I'd found that silence could sometimes be your best defense. "Gabby said that if we could get in here, then it'd open her up to new clients and she'd continue to make the money she'd been making."

"Why would Leah want to kill her?" I questioned.

"Gabby said that Leah was going to start selling Lifestyle in Whispering Falls. Gabby told her over her dead body. At the time we laughed about it, but not so much now." Her face hardened. "There was something else." She scratched her head. "But I can't remember."

There was a bit of relief that settled over me hoping the spell put over Beth had left Beth without the memory of Gabby seeing Leah doing magic, if she even did.

Her phone rang and she looked at it. She held a finger up to me and answered it.

"Listen, I know I owe you money," there was anger in her voice.

While she argued with the person on the other end of her phone call, I clearly remember Gabby saying that to whoever she was talking to on the phone when I walked in on her at Crafty Crazy Chick that day, that they were going to have to go through her dead body or something similar to that. Leah LeRoy had told me she was at Wicked Good Bakery with Raven during that time, so I didn't think it was Leah on the other end of Gabby's phone call. It was something I could easily check out.

"You'll have your payment by the end of the week." Beth let out a deep sigh and pushed the phone back in her pocket. "Bill collector. I'm late on my car payment." She rolled her eyes. "Anyways, when we first became reps for Lifestyle, we had no idea how much money we were going to make. I guess I'll be taking over her clients." The sudden shift in her in mood didn't go unnoticed.

"I know that Leah is now arrested, but did Gabby have a client list or maybe some clients that weren't happy with the product that couldn't've had a beef with her?" I questioned.

"She does have a client list that I can forward to you because it's on our national sales email." She pulled her phone out. "What's your email and I'll send it to you?"

I quickly spout off my email and couldn't believe she was so forthcoming.

"I guess now you'll get the number one sales position with Gabby's clients. She told me she made six-figures." I wanted to know Beth's thoughts on this because I couldn't help but think with Gabby out of the way, Beth would be happy to take the money. Especially now that I knew she had some financial issues.

"Poor Gabby, she told me that it was only her and she didn't have anyone to rely on but I wonder who the father of her baby was," I said because things weren't as black and white as Beth was making it appear to be.

"Baby?" Beth's face jerked up, her jaw dropped. "What baby?"

"Gabby was pregnant. I thought since you two were best friends that you knew." My intuition bells dinged loud and clear.

The beautiful brightly colored freckles on Beth's face, turned flesh color and she paled.

"I've got to go." She jumped up and grabbed her purse. "I'll have to come back another time."

I guess Gabby didn't tell her everything. My eyes narrowed as I watched her rush out of the police station.

"What was that about? Where is she going? I need her statement." Oscar didn't sound too happy that Beth had left.

"I'm not so sure just how good of friends Beth and Gabby were as much as co-workers with a bit of jealousy between them," I whispered and turned to Oscar. "Beth had no idea Gabby was pregnant and she got a phone call from a bill collector."

"Interesting." Oscar slowly nodded his head. "It looks like we need to dig a little deeper into Beth Phipps."

"And I've got just the answer to watch her." I smiled and then looked out the window over at Happy Herb.

Chapter Eighteen

If I was going to get to the shop in time to open, I knew I wasn't going to have much time to visit with KJ, though I truly wanted too. He was such a special friend to me. His father, Kenny, had been my connection to the Native American village when I moved to Whispering Falls and my go-to when I needed a special herb from their native land.

Kenny had befriended Darla and it was a special bond that connected me to him. Now that his son has taken his job after Kenny had died, it left the two of us with a bond.

My inside joy shone on the bright smile of my face when I looked at Happy Herb. I slipped my shoes off my feet when I reached the gate and tucked them up under one arm, holding the extra soufflé I'd gotten Colton.

The walkway up to the shop was made of the prettiest Kentucky Bluegrass with stepping stones. It was a shame not to feel the fluffy strands between my toes. Darla always told me to feel the grass under my feet and this was one time I was going to.

When I got to the top of the steps, I put a hand on the grass door and pushed it open using the bamboo handle, stepping inside.

Of course I could buy rosemary, ginger, sage, lavender, and the unforgettable smell of cinnamon from a store, but it was KJ's special mixture that brought my potions to life.

"June." KJ's baritone voice greeted me. "I've been expecting you."

"You have?" I walked across the grassy floor of his herb shop and held out the bag. "I brought you some breakfast."

"I've got you some black locust." He held the package in exchange for my soufflé. "How did you know?" I asked knowing that I didn't whisper into the air.

Before KJ moved here from the Native American village out west and was in need of ingredient refills for my potions, I whispered what I needed into the night air. My words and order would travel across the miles into KJ's ears. It took no time at all for KJ to show up at A Charming Cure with exactly what I needed and sometimes something I didn't know I needed but would soon have a purpose for it.

"When I heard there was a death next door, I sat in silence." He stood over six-foot-four. Last night he had on his traditional loin cloth for the smudge but today he wore a pair of khaki pants, button down shirt, but still had on the feather headdress. "The curse of the black locust whispered to me."

"You should be a police officer." I half joked but half told the truth. "The Karima sisters said the young woman had it in her system due to this roll-on oil she sold. I came here to ask you about the seeds. I'm not very familiar with them and I am helping out Oscar."

"Maybe you need to be the officer," he suggested and winked. "Follow me back here." KJ's dark eyes looked down at me. "I'm still refilling the men's section. The customers wiped me out yesterday."

"It was a good sales day." I agreed. "From what I understand, the seeds have to be really crushed and mixed," I continued to talk to him because I had to hurry up since it was almost opening up time and I'd yet to get to Hidden Hall.

I followed him through the shop and felt like I was in the woods. The walls were painted with green ivy stems to go with the herb theme.

It appeared he had been restocking the natural wood shelving in the men's health section because there was product sitting all over the grass. I was hoping he needed help with the women's section since I rarely got to come over to shop.

"I sent a lot of customers your way yesterday." He opened the bag and took the soufflé out, lifting it to his nose.

"Thank you. It was a much-needed boost. It smells good, and tastes even better." I was glad to bring him the treat.

"I'm getting the feeling that you have more than just questions about the black locust seed to have come visited, though I am happy to see you." He was so smart and cleaver.

"I wanted to rent an owl." It was a rare request but if you needed a spy, Native Americans had the best connections. "Leah LeRoy didn't kill that girl, though I know Oscar wants it to appear that way." Without giving too many details, I gave him a summarizion of Beth Phipps and why I needed to track her.

"She appeared to be upset when she heard the news of the baby?" He questioned. "How far along was the deceased?"

"I don't know those small details. The only thing I can go on was how my intuition reacted to Beth when I told her about the baby. She was definitely upset. Plus, she had that phone call about the bill collector." I picked up a few of his bottles and started to restock the shelves while he enjoyed the last few bites of his soufflé. "I'm not saying that she killed Gabby. I'm just saying she knows more than she wants to tell. She was quick to point the finger at Leah, even though Gabby did catch Leah doing magic."

"And you don't think Leah, who did buy the seeds from me, didn't use them against Gabby to keep her quiet?" He questioned Leah's honesty and loyalty to the village. "You and I both know that if something like this happens, she was to go immediately to the village president and apparently she didn't." He wadded up the bag and shot it in the air like a basketball player, making it into the trash can next to the counter where the customers paid for their products. "What exactly do you want my owl to do?"

"I only want to know her whereabouts for the next twenty-four hours. I want to see who she goes to see and if they have any connections to Gabby. She left in such a hurry, I felt like she was going to meet someone. If this is the case, then we'd have another suspect and Leah could get back into her shop since she's not allowed to work until the investigation is over." I put the last bottle on the shelf and looked up at the clock on his wall. "Her name is Beth Phipps."

KJ only needed the name to bring her up in the spiritual world and communicate that information with the owl of his choosing.

"I've got to run to Hidden Hall before we open, so just let me know what you decide." I hugged him. "I understand if you don't think this is an appropriate job for your creatures."

"Don't be ridiculous." He looked down at me. "I know you wouldn't ask if you didn't truly need it."

His words were assurance enough that he was going to take care of what I asked him to do.

"Also," he called after me when I turned to leave, "in the envelop of the seeds, you'll find the side effects and uses of the black locust."

Chapter Nineteen

Hidden Hall, the Spiritualist University, wasn't anywhere near Whispering Falls. It was one of those magic portals the mortals were always trying to find. If they only knew that these portals weren't like being zapped into another world. It was actually as simple as just touching the right thing to change the environment in front of you.

To get to the portal, I had to walk up the hill past the gathering rock. Once I was up there, I looked over my shoulder and gazed over Whispering Falls. Even though there was something hanging over the village, my heart swelled with the warm feeling of how much I loved Whispering Falls. It was my home and if I were to take a teaching position, then I'd really miss it.

Meow, meow.

Mr. Prince Charming caused me to turn back towards the rock and look at the wooded area. I heard him, but all I could see was his white tail dancing along the trail, leading the way to the wheat field where the portal was located.

Even in the season, the wheat field was tall and shiny with long arms of the flowering stems that swayed to the right and swayed to the left in a perfect dance. A with several long wooden arms, each with a finger pointing in a different direction, was located in the middle and that's where I found Mr. Prince Charming waiting for me.

Each arm had a different school for the University. I tapped the one that said Intuition school and smiled as the wheat parted and a perfect golden train began to trickle out in front of me.

Mr. Prince Charming didn't even wait for me. He darted in as the path gained momentum. I took my time to enjoy the beautiful weather the University was having and trying to really tap into my feelings about the overall position I was in. It took a lot for me to put what was going on in Whispering Falls in the back of my head so I could focus on my future.

Before I knew it, I was standing in front of the small yellow cottage with an awning that flapped in the light breeze that read Intuition School in lime green calligraphy. The window boxes under each window overflowed with Geraniums, Morning Glories, Petunias, Moon Flowers, and Trailing Ivy a rainbow of colorful explosions. It always looked vibrant and smelled so fragrant.

Curling up on the tips of my toes, I looked into the window. Aunt Helena was busy grinding something up using the mortar and pestle. She added it to the copper cauldron along with a dash of topaz globules, some mandrake flakes, and cobalt root.

The room of young witches looked at her with a gleam and awe in their eyes. A few of them gasped when the tiny firework show over the cauldron displayed with some booms and pops. When the show was over, there were some giggles and claps. She ran her hands down her A-line dress before folding them together as her body swayed back and forth in a delightful fluid motion.

Aunt Helena must've felt me there, because she glanced over her shoulder and looked at me with a smile before gesturing me to come in.

"Now, now," she clapped and instructed the girls, "settle down. We've got a very important visitor."

All the eyes were on me.

"My Great-Niece June Heal and her fairy-god cat, Mr. Prince Charming have come all the way from Whispering Falls, Kentucky. Let's make sure we are all on our good behavior while she's here." She snapped her fingers and the girls went back to what they'd been working on in their personal cauldrons in front of them.

"I'm sorry I interrupted," I apologized because I knew how much of a stickler Aunt Helena really was.

"Don't be ridiculous." There was an underlying meaning to that grin across her lips. "I'd love for you to see what the future is doing and how you can have a hand in shaping that future."

"Really, I had to come to get cauldron cleaner from Wands, Potions, and Beyond. You just happen to be the first stop on the way."

"You, June Heal, cannot fool your aunt who is a spiritualist." She tsked and dragged her hand out in front of her. "Why don't you just take a minute to walk around and chat with the girls. You'll be surprised."

It wasn't a bad idea. If I were to take the job, it would be in this very room that I'd teach.

There were two rows of wooden top tables with two students per table. They each had a stool on which to sit and a cauldron in front of them. Aunt Helena's desk was in the front of the room and her cauldron was much bigger. There was a bookshelf behind her desk that held test tubes, potion bottles, ingredients and some reference books among other witchy things.

Mr. Prince Charming teased and flirted with all the girls as he jumped from table to table and dragged his tail underneath their noses, tickling them into a fit of giggles.

I walked up and down the aisle with my hands clasped behind my back, listening to the girls discuss how each one of them had different intuitions on how to fix it.

"Yes, I understand you have the warmth here." The young woman with the chin length hair cut that was shorter in the back and longer in the front in a very stylish kind of way, insisted she was right. "When you read someone, you can't just say I feel a warmth here. You have to go deeper and see exactly what the warmth means. Is it a heart condition? A break up? A loss of something? You have to hone in on the gift."

"But it's the heart. I know it's the heart. The glow is around the chamber." The other girl debated with her. When she jutted her head back and forth, her long pony tail swung around like a propeller.

"Hi there," I greeted both of them. "I don't mean to interrupt your debate but have you ever thought that you are both right?" I asked.

The two looked at each other and then back at me, shaking their heads.

"In here it's easy to think that it's only one thing or the other, but out there, mortals always have a way of multi-tasking. This means there can be multiple things in their system. So this particular person you are trying to get a good potion for could be experiencing heartache from a loss that can lead into bad health in which would be a heart condition like a heart attack." I knew it wasn't as simple as what I was saying and had to give some examples.

"Exactly what do we go on to make a potion?" The brunette was very interested, more so than the girl with the pony tail.

"What's your name?" I asked.

"I'm Erika Minter from the East Village." Her bright hazel eyes had a flick of interest. I could tell she really was there to learn and excel in your spiritual profession.

"What is it that you'd like to do when you graduate?" I asked.

"I'd like to be a doctor like they have in the hospital here. Help out my people." She was an ambitious one.

"That's a very good profession and we could use a lot more doctors." I wanted to give her some encouragement.

It was from my past experience and being thrown into my gift as an adult that I felt like I missed out on a mentor. These girls were young, and they could be shaped and molded.

"I can only speak from experience as a shop owner and because all my customers come in for a reason. They might think they have a heart condition." I looked at the other girl and then back at Erika. "But in reality it's the heart ache of something lost."

I leaned over the cauldron and looked inside at the translucent, thin potion that was ivory in color. I lifted my finger to my nose to shield it from the black pepper and fish smell. I stuck the tip of my finger in and put a little of the potion on my finger, bringing it to my tongue. The taste of blueberry hit my gut and the vision of a happy couple blueberry picking played like a reel in my head. I steadied myself as I watched the few seconds of the scene play out in my head.

"It might smell a little strange, but it tastes like blueberry." I was happy to work with them. "Blueberries carry antioxidants that's a heart healthy fruit. This person definitely has a heart condition but from a break up." Both girls looked at each other and then back at me with dipped brows. "Say you are my customer or my patient, I would walk over to you and ask you about your day. Let's role play," I suggested to Erika.

"Good morning, how are you today?" I reached out and touched her. "Now, by me touching you, I'm starting to get in tune with my intuition."

"I see." She nodded eagerly. "I'm just looking around," she played along.

"I see that you're interested in the low stress lotions." I pretended to pick out a bottle from the air. "Lavender is wonderful."

"Yes. Good for sleep." She was doing a great job pretending. "I'm not sleeping well because I've got a little bit of indigestion."

"I'm sorry to hear that but I might have something you can use." I touched her back and pretend to guide her in the other direction. "See what I did there? I touched your arm at first and didn't get a connection, then as you talked and said you had indigestion, I touched your back to get to the core of your person and guided you to the side where my indigestion and heart products would be in my shop."

"So you interact with them and interpret their words while touching them in different areas." It was like a light bulb went off.

"Yes. And my intuition is how I know what is really bothering them. In this case," I gestured to the cauldron, "this person needed a heart potion which you both established. So very good for that, but you have to dig deeper into your intuition to get to the root of their problem. When the potion tasted like blueberry, I got a sense of how much blueberry meant to this client and how as a couple, they picked blueberries together."

"I see." Her hazel eyes opened wide.

"Now," I brought her back into the pretend play. "Try this one." I pretend to put lotion on her hand. "Do you have a significant other?"

"I did, but he died." She continued to play along.

"I'm so sorry to hear that." I continued to pretend to rub the lotion on her hand. "Do you like this smell? It's a hint of blueberry."

"Oh, now your tapping into the story you felt in your intuition." Erika snapped.

"Right." I smiled when I realized she'd really gotten to the root of the potion and mixing. "This is how you will make a potion just for her. She's desperately saddened. Not sleeping because of the heartache, not indigestion."

"That's how we know what ingredients to use in her personal care." The other girl spoke up and reached for some different ingredients to throw into the cauldron. "You're good."

"Thanks," I said.

It did feel good that they were starting to understand the power of really tapping into their gift. I decided it was time to let them finish on their own and took a couple of steps forward.

Little did I realize the entire class was looking at me and listening to my analogy. When I looked up to continue walking around the room, I noticed them and the pride glowing on Aunt Helena's face.

"You are a sneaky one," I said when I walked up to her.

"I just wanted you to see how much you have to offer these girls. I don't have the young, vibrant teaching skills anymore and we need younger, talented women like you." She scanned the room. All the girls were busy at their work stations. "June, we could really use you and I think you'll get so much more out of it than the good pay."

Mr. Prince Charming darted off one of the desks and scurried over to the door.

"I've got to go. I'm limited on time, but I'll think about it." I gave her a quick hug before Mr. Prince Charming and I rushed into the core of the University.

Like all mortal Universities, Hidden Hall was no different. There was an active greek life, restaurants, bars, many old buildings, students rushing around, and bicyclists barely missing me.

"I heard through the breeze you were here." The familiar voice of Gus Chatham came up from behind me.

"Gus!" I turned and threw my arms around him. "Look at you."

"I'm all grown up with a man cut." He laughed. Long gone was his shaggy head of hair and baggy surfer dude clothes. He actually had on a wizard hat and cape. "I've been teaching."

"You have?" I curled my arm into the crook of his arm as we continued to walk down the street. "I'm so proud of you. So, you're not Aunt Helena's assistant anymore?"

"Oh yeah. I'm that too. We are so shorthanded. Now that the villages have opened up to mortals and neighborhoods, spiritualists want more freedom and not to teach the young. Look." He nodded towards the ornery shaggy dog coming towards us.

"Elroy!" I bent down and put my arms around the cuddly crystal ball spiritualist that come back in dog form.

"He's even back to teach." Gus gave him a good scratch.

Mr. Prince Charming and Elroy seemed to be connecting on some sort of animal level, so Gus and I didn't bother them. Elroy was so darn cute with his small turban on his head and the necklaces of bead around his neck.

Hidden Hall was a very special place and all of my friends here made me feel so welcomed.

"I did hear that you were extended an invitation to teach next semester and I can only hope that's why you are here?" He patted my hand.

I squeezed his arm.

"I think Aunt Helena must've put you up to greeting me." I winked and stopped as soon as we got to the front of Wands, Potions and Beyond. "I'm thinking about it, but I'm still a newlywed and have the shop and all."

"That's minor details. It's not like you can't go home to see him." He rolled his eyes and let out a long sigh.

"What about your heritage? Your family? We'll be extinct if you don't help."

"I doubt that." I gave him one last hug. "I've got to get my cleaner and head back to Whispering Falls before it's time to open my shop."

He placed both of his hands on my shoulders and stared into my eyes.

"June, please, I beg you to consider taking the teaching position. The deadline is next week before they extend it to someone else," his voice held concern. "No one is as good as you and no one can motivate these young girls to carry on like a vibrant and hip witch like you."

"Flattery will get you everywhere." I joked and hugged my sweet friend one last time before I headed into the store.

Wands, Potions, and Beyond was somewhere I could get lost in for hours, not to mention spend all my money. It was one of those places that I walked in to get one thing but walked out with a million more items that I truly didn't need.

There were aisle and aisle of ingredients, potions, bottles, wands, clothing, and different things sold exclusively from different villages. It was tempting to buy the latest model cauldron but I knew mine was nice and seasoned, so I hurried away from them so I wouldn't change my mind and stopped in the next aisle over where the cleaner was located.

"I swear I smell June Heal."

I turned and looked up the aisle.

"Tilly, my friend." We started to walk towards each other and met in the middle. We hugged and asked how each other had been doing.

"I see your hair is still amazingly purple." I was always jealous of her free-bird style attitude.

"I'll never change." Her white eyes glowed. "What on earth are you doing here so early?"

"I need cauldron cleaner." I pointed to the shelf.

"June," she tsked, drumming her black tipped fingernails on the cleaner bottle. "Don't you know that we sale the latest in self-cleaning cauldrons." Her head tilted. "It's the latest rage."

"I'm good. I like to care for my own." I grabbed a bottle.

"I hear there's a bit of trouble in Whispering Falls." She led the way to the front of the store so I could check out. "What's going on?"

"A spiritualist from Atlanta was accused of killing a mortal. How did you hear?" I pulled the money out of my bag.

"The Order of Elders were here to work on the shortage of professors and they had to go out west for something, then changed their plans to head your way." She warned.

"It doesn't look good, but I told her I'd help her because I know she didn't do it. Though the gal that was murdered did see her do some magic and I think she told her mortal friends about it." I shrugged.

"Are there any other suspects?" Tilly asked.

Tilly had always been such a good ear to lean on during my time at Hidden Hall and she'd been able to offer some really good insight on my relationship with Aunt Helena. She had a tendency to look at things in a different way.

"There is this one girl that claims to be Gabby's best friend." I quickly told her about Beth and about Nina. "When I asked Beth who the father of Gabby's baby was, she took off. Do you know KJ?"

"Yes." She nodded. "Tall, dark, handsome, and good at what he does."

"That's the one." I winked. "He opened Happy Herb in Whispering Falls and he's sent an owl into Locust Grove to follow Beth. I'm curious to see who she talks too and if she can lead me to anyone who else might know Gabby."

"You mentioned that Nina left you business card." Her eyes narrowed. "Not that I want to put you in danger, but why don't you go see her and try to be a consultant and see what you find out."

"Me?" I laughed.

"Why not?" She drew back. "You don't need the job, but you could you know." She twirled her finger in the air. "Use a spell or two to get a party together."

"Or I could see if Gabby already had a party lined up and just fill in." I shrugged and thought that sounded like a good idea. "I just don't have time to get a full client list because of the Marys. Gabby called on the Marys the night Oscar questioned her."

"I heard something about that." She gave me a sympathetic look.

"Oh no." Gossip in the spiritual world was just as bad as in the mortal world.

"Whatever you decide to do, you better hurry up because I overheard that their mission in the west village was going fast and would be wrapped up a day early." She handed me the bag with the cleaner in it.

"A day early?" I gasped and rubbed my bracelet. "Bye!"

I rushed out the door and met Mr. Prince Charming.

"We've got to hurry up and get back. We've only got twenty-four hours to figure out who killed Gabby before the Elders shut us down," I told him as we ran into the direction of the wheat field.

Chapter Twenty

The thought of taking over Gabby's parties on a temporary basis, though I wouldn't tell Nina that, did roll around in my head on my way back to Whispering Falls. It wasn't like I had to work too hard to know what was in the product. I could even put a little spell in them to make them want to come see me and I'd let them know where I was located. It was a win for me investigating the case and getting business up.

Too bad it was too close to opening time by the time I got to A Charming Cure. The visit to Nina would have to wait.

"Leah." I was a little stunned to see her sitting on the step of the shop. "What's going on?"

"I wanted to bring you these papers before it got too messy in here when the Order of Elders arrive. I'd rather you get a look at them first." She shook her head and rolled her eyes. "I really do wish that I didn't call my parents that night."

I put my hand on her arm for a little comfort.

"First off, you're very lucky that you have parents who can give you advice." My eyes softened as I smiled at her. I could feel her body start to release the stress underneath my fingertips. "Secondly, you're here. You're learning your way in the world and if there was a next time you get in trouble, which I'm sure there won't be, then you'll know what to do instead of running home. You're growing up."

"You always have the right words." She gave me a quick hug.

"Come on in." I moved past her and put the skeleton key in the door, unlocking and flipping on the lights once inside. "We can chat about some things I've found out."

"Really?" There was a peek of interest in her tone.

I flipped the sign to open and took a quick look outside to see if Mr. Prince Charming was around then realized I was so caught up in my thoughts on the way back, I didn't even notice which way he went. With a quick feel of my bracelet, I sucked in a deep breath of the morning air and shut the door.

"I'll put these papers on your counter." Leah walked to the back of the shop and I walked over to the chalkboard to change the daily special, but when I was reminded about the baby potions, I decided to keep it up there.

"Did you know that Gabby was pregnant?" I asked and headed behind the counter.

"No. She always said she was tired, but I had no idea." Leah sat on the stool next to the counter. "I didn't know much about her. Like I said, I went to one of those parties and she came to my shop. Once she saw my little bags, it was her that wanted to collaborate. I figured it'd be a good idea. Boy was I wrong."

"So just to be clear." I reached underneath the counter to grab the cookies from Wicked Good to go on the hospitality table for the customers. "You two made a deal. On the whim, you agreed to get your name out in Locust Grove or with her customers by making the bags. In turn, you agreed to host a Lifestyle party," I said on the way over to the table to arrange the cookies and turn on the cauldron of warm tea.

"That's right. And after I got to know you and the rest of the village, I knew I'd made a mistake and I couldn't just worry about myself anymore." She fiddled with her fingers.

"See, you're growing up. When you become a village member, you realize that you've got to look out for everyone." I felt like I was teaching her and it reminded me of the time I'd spent with the young witches this morning at Hidden Hall.

"I just wish I could take it all back. When she walked in on me, I was trying to do a spell in the bags that would make her forget our deal," her voice fell away.

"Let's take a look at these papers." I didn't want to beat her mistake into the ground. It wasn't anyway for her to learn her mistake. It was just time to move forward as quickly as we could.

"Are you sure you have time this morning?" She asked.

"Of course I do." I dragged them to me and flipped to the last page to see what lawyer had put them together. "I don't recognize this name."

"You know a lot of lawyers?" she asked.

"I grew up in Locust Grove and so did Oscar. We didn't move here until we were adults." I left out our age since we were just newly considered adults. "It's not a big town, but I've been gone a few years."

"Even if you did know the lawyer, what does that matter?" She leaned over the counter and looked at the name I was pointing to.

"I would go see them and tell them this was ridiculous." I tapped the name and my eyes drew over to Nina Teeter's business card that was resting on the keys of the cash register. "I wonder if this is the lawyer for Lifestyle?"

"I can't believe that she'd sue me." Leah let out a nervous laughter. "It says right here that she's going to sue me for liability and defamation."

"The liability is because of your bag in the hands of her customers. And if something happened to a customer with your bag, not that something bad could happen, but her insurance wouldn't pay for it since you didn't hold up on your end of the deal. The defamation is that you're gaining customers because you're using her name and product to get your product into their hands." I hated to say it, but it looked pretty binding. "This alone would be enough for a prosecutor, a mortal one," I was sure to point out because this was a mortal we were dealing with, "to say that you killed her out of passion. It's the black locust seed poisoning that makes it look like murder one, pre-meditation."

"So you're telling me that you found out nothing to help me and I'm in big trouble." She gulped and pushed her brown hair behind her shoulder. "And my only hope is the Order of Elders?"

"Not at all. I do have a suspicion that Gabby's best friend might have a motive, but I've got to go to Locust Grove to check out a few things." I grabbed the business card and stared at it. "I don't want to burden you with the details because you already have a lot on your plate, but the rules never stated that you can't work in a shop in the village, you just can't work in your shop or perform your gift."

"What are you saying?" Her head swung to the side and she looked at me with a suspicious look.

"What are you doing today?" I tucked the business card in my back pocket and grabbed my bag, strapping it across my body.

"Whatever you need me to do," her words dragged out in a mysterious way.

"I want you to work for me here today. If someone needs something special, there's box in the back room that has Piggly Wiggly written on it. It's its own magical bottle for clients. So just sell them one of those. Other than that, just answer the phone and take the money." I darted around the counter and across the shop floor. "I've got an idea.

Don't tell anyone where I'm at. Just tell them I had some business to take care of."

Without another word, I scurried out the door and up the hill to my house not surprised to see Mr. Prince Charming was already on the dashboard, curled up and waiting for me. I had no idea how he got in there and didn't care. There was a nip in the air that told me the Elders were closer than I cared for them to be.

The drive to Locust Grove took thirty minutes along curvy and windy roads. I knew them like the back of my hand and the closer I got to the Locust Grove border, the heavier my foot got on the pedal. Though this was a trip on business, it always filled me up from the bit homesickness that I was used to feeling since I moved to Whispering Falls.

The house that Darla and I lived in and I still own, was just inside the city limits and I had to pass it on my way into town. Oscar's house was right across the street and the big tree we use to spend hours under eating Ding Dongs was still there. We still owned the houses, but we rented them out. It was nice to see the pulse of the houses, alive and happy with the new tenants and their children.

As much as I'd like to say that houses were just houses, I had to believe there was a little magic in the walls, carpet and roof to keep them safe and happy.

I slowed down to get a good look at them as we passed without stopping completely. It was the only time Mr. Prince Charming had looked up from his slumber.

Meow. Meow. He looked at me.

"Yeah, I miss it too." I gave a flat smile and gripped the wheel before pushing the toe of my shoe down on the pedal and speeding off into town.

Chapter Twenty-One

I pulled the Green Machine into the strip mall parking lot and double-checked the address on Nina's card. It didn't appear to be that big of a company. Anyway, I put the car in park.

"Are you coming?" I asked.

Mr. Prince Charming stretched out his front legs and dug his claws into the dash, letting out a big yawn before he decided to get up.

"Let's go." I opened the door, letting him run across me and jump out.

The door didn't even have a sign on it, just the address. I double-checked the card again. It was the right place according to what was printed on there. I slipped it back into my pocket and tugged open the door.

Inside was a different story. There was a receptionist on the phone with a room filled with cardboard boxes. While I waited for her to get off the phone, I walked around and looked at the labels. It had the Lifestyle logo and some of them had Gabby's name on them.

"I'm not sure about the party, ma'am," the receptionist was talking to the person. "We had no idea that she was going to pass away. But if you hold on a second, I'll check with her boss."

I looked over at her.

"Hi." She held up a finger to me. "I'll be with you in a minute." She jabbed a button on her phone. "Nina, I have a very angry customer on the phone and she said that Gabby was supposed to do a party at lunch. She's got a lot of local business owners and even someone with a tie to a big perfume chain coming. What can we do?"

Before I could even turn back around, I heard a door slam followed up by heavy footsteps coming from the only hallway in the place. Suddenly, Nina Teeter appeared.

"June." She looked between me and the receptionist. "You didn't tell me June was here." Her face stilled and grew serious when she looked at the receptionist.

"I just walked in." I held out my hand for her to shake.

"We don't allow animals in here in case of allergies with clients." She took my hand but her eyes were focused on Mr. Prince Charming who was currently taking advantage of her dislike of cats by doing figure eights around her ankles.

"It's a therapy thing." I lied knowing that I couldn't just blurt out that I was a witch that did real potions to help people and he was my fairy-god cat.

"Oh." She pulled her hand away. "If you give me one minute. I've got something to take care of."

"Actually," I said and stepped in between her and the receptionist desk. "I overheard the conversation and I was here to let you know that I'd like to give this a shot. Selling your product. I promise I know a lot about oils and obviously you've seen my shop. If I could do a trial party, then we can sit down tomorrow and discuss me being a consultant under you and possibly getting a display in my shop in Whispering Falls."

"I don't know." She acted as though she were playing hardball, but deep in my gut I knew the thought of getting into a shop in Whispering Falls was exactly what she and Gabby had been trying to do with Leah.

"It helps us out even if it's only one time," the receptionist chimed in and gave Nina the big-eyed look, like she better jump on my offer.

Nina let out a big sigh. She stared at me with an open mouth, the tip of her tongue played with her back teeth as her mouth contorted.

"What's the worse thing that can happen? They buy me out?" I laughed.

"Fine," Nina said with stiffness in her tone. "Angie, get her the directions and one of the new consultant bags."

"A new product box?" Angie called after Nina.

"No." She looked at me. "Give her what Gabby was using. Might as well get rid of her stock."

"Sounds good." Angie clicked back on the phone and told the customer that June, a consultant would be there in under an hour to set up and start.

They hung up and she got up out of her chair. She walked over to the closet and took out a package.

"Here is the new consultant bag." She took the package back to her desk and ripped it open. She took out a bag with the Lifestyle logo on it. Also, inside the package were samples of the products. "We are featuring the new summer line, though it's not technically summer." She took out a brochure type paper and flattened it out. "Here is how we'd like for you to make your display on the table. You don't have to, but we've found it best that the products are seen while doing a presentation."

"Got it." I nodded.

"Let me get Gabby's leftover products." She hurried down the hall where Nina had appeared then disappeared back in to.

I put all the products from the package into the bag while I waited for her.

"These are cash and carry oils. They can either order the product or take what we have." She handed over a big box. "Obviously, we want you to push these products to get them out of inventory."

"I guess I better get going." I looked at her over the top of the box. "I just need the address of the client."

"No problem." She walked back to her desk and scribbled something on a post it note before she came back and smacked it on the top of the box. "If you have any issues, my number is on there."

"Okay." I nodded. "Can you get the door for me?"

"When you are done, you need to call me with the sales numbers," she instructed me and held the door open. "Got it?"

"Got it." I walked out and couldn't help but smile. This had gone much better than I thought.

Mr. Prince Charming jumped up on the hood of the El Camino. I sat the box on the ground and opened the car door. The box for Adeline at the Piggly Wiggly, that Faith was unable to deliver for me, was in the floorboard, so I stuck the new box of Lifestyle on the seat and we got in.

Rowl, rowl! Mr. Prince Charming batted at the post it note. I picked it up and read it.

"Oh no," I groaned when I noticed it was Adeline's name and the Piggly Wiggly. "This was her favor to me."

I crumbled the note up in my hand and threw it on the ground.

"Well, it looks like we can kill two birds with one stone. I'll drop off our potions and then give her the news about Gabby. Not all is lost." I started the engine. "At least Nina might give me another one of Gabby's parties so I can get in with some insight."

Mewl, mewl. His tail tapped the lawsuit papers of Leah's that was sitting on the seat.

"No. I didn't figure out if this is the Lifestyle lawyer," I informed him since he wasn't happy I'd taken this job so quickly. "Listen, I saw the opportunity and took it. How was I to know that it was for Adeline?"

He took his tail and tapped the tip of it to my bag. Like an x-ray machine, Madame Torres light up inside.

"Alright." I put my hands up in the air before I pulled down on the gear shift. "I should've asked her first." I gripped the wheel and gave him a quick glance. "Since when did you two become friends?"

He batted my bracelet that was dangling from my wrist.

"Okay. I get it." I sucked in a deep breath and headed towards the Piggly Wiggly.

On our way over, my phone rang.

"Oscar, you aren't going to believe what I'm doing." I answered the phone and immediately started talking.

"No. You aren't going to believe what I'm going to tell you." His news sounded much more important than my little undercover scheme.

"What? You're scaring me." I sucked in a deep breath, ready for the hit of whatever he was about to say.

"Sonny, you know my buddy from the Locust Grove Sheriff's department?" He paused.

"Yeah. You used to work with him." They were partners before Oscar took the job in Whispering Falls.

"He's got the go ahead on the Gabby Summerfied case. It appears her boss went to the police. She also told him about Leah LeRoy and how there was some evidence and a witness that Leah had motive to kill her. Since it's across the county line, the judge ruled a warrant for them to come to Whispering Falls and do what was necessary to aide in the investigation." This was the worst news other than the Order of Elders.

"This means that we can't do any more magic to try to get the answers." My passion on figuring out who really killed Gabby had just intensified, not only for Leah's sake, but now Whispering Falls was going to be in the spotlight and that was never good for a spiritualist world.

Chapter Twenty-Two

"June." Adeline greeted me.

I'd found her in the employee break room in the back of the Piggly Wiggly.

"Let me help you with that." She hurried over when she noticed I had the box of my product from A Charming Cure. "Your friend will be here soon to give a presentation to some of my managers and a few friends."

"About that." I followed her to the stock room where she had me put the box on a shelf with my name printed on it. "Gabby Summerfield has been murdered."

I pushed the box on the shelf and turned to face a stunned Adeline.

"Yeah. I figured you'd react that way, but," I knew she was going to think I was nuts. "you know that I've stuck my nose in a case or two."

"June, no." She shook her head. "Don't tell me you're looking into who killed her."

"I won't tell you then." My words met with her pacing back and forth. "Just listen." I put my hand out to stop her from walking a hole in her floor. "I'm helping Oscar out on this one and I've got some good leads. Only it means that I have to do her show for you today."

"What?" Adeline's jaw dropped. "Her product isn't nearly as good as yours and I was only doing this as a favor."

"I understand that and I'm prepared with a plan where you don't have to purchase a thing," I assured her.

"This is ridiculous." Adeline wasn't happy. "I don't even have space in any of my grocery stores for her product. Let me just make a few phone calls."

"Don't do that," I assured her. "Just let me do the presentation and that way, it gets my foot in the door for Oscar."

She stood there for a minute. I could tell she was contemplating.

"You know, I could call her friend Beth," she said, getting my full attention.

"How do you know Beth?" I asked.

"She came in here saying that Gabby had told her that she had her foot in the door here. Beth said that she'd be willing to undercut Gabby's prices if I cancelled Gabby and had her do the presentation instead." Her word sent my intuition into a tailspin. "Do you need a Ding Dong?"

"Yes." I nodded and melted down on the floor in cross-legged position.

Mr. Prince Charming stood in front of me, dragging his tail underneath my nose. Sometimes when I got dizzy and my gift took over my body, as it was doing now, the tickle of his tail brought me back.

"This is just another thing that makes Beth have motive," I told him and ran my hand down his fur.

He purred in delight. My bag warmed to my leg. Madame Torres glowed, her light shot out of the bag like a beam. I pulled her out and put her up to my face.

"Look deep into the depths of the raging water to see." The glass ball swirled with a deep pink. "It'll be me you seek and be. The mix of smells will bring you closure, but not until a few days will be over." Madame Torres said the exact same thing she'd said to me a couple of days ago.

"It's been a few days," I said to her. "Does this mean that I'm right? Is it Beth that killed Gabby out of jealousy?" I asked the raging ball and watched as the pink deepened and deepened into a crimson with black ribbons running through it until the black got bigger and took up more space, leaving the entire ball black.

"Here you go." Adeline handed me a box of Ding Dongs. "Just eat them all. You look like you could use a few. Have you been eating lately?"

"I'm fine." I pushed Madame Torres back into my bag so Adeline wouldn't ask any questions. I opened one of the tasty treats and practically shoved the entire thing in my mouth, letting the chocolate seep into my soul, causing me to take deep breaths and calm my nerves.

"Now, why don't I call Beth," Adeline suggested.

Deep down, I knew that the owl KJ had sent to watch Beth was watching her every move. So whether or not I did the show, I'd know where she was if she did the show. It would buy me some time to take my facts back to Oscar and see what he thought.

"Are you sure?" I asked.

"Positive." She nodded. "Let's go back to my office and get her number."

Adeline helped me up and once we got back to her office, she called Beth, who was all too eager to get the opportunity.

Before we could barely restock my product on the Piggly Wiggly shelf, Beth was there and not alone. She had a helper. I continued to stock my product since I had to put the final touches of magic on them and it was in the contract that I was the one to place the product on the shelf because I told her that I was the only one who knew the order. In reality, I just had to touch each one before they made their way out into the mortal world.

The man carried in her boxes of product and followed Adeline to the back into the employee room where she'd already set up the tables for Gabby.

"Will that be all?" he asked and caught my attention.

I leaned around the aisle my product was in and took at look at him.

My world went completely black after I zeroed in on the white eyebrow.

"June. June." I could hear Adeline's voice, but had to blink several times before she came into focus. "That's it. Look at me."

"I'm. . .I'm . . ." I sat straight up when I realized what'd happened. "I think you're right. I've not been eating good lately."

Behind her stood Beth and the man.

"I think you know Beth." Adeline looked over her shoulder. "At least she said she met you at the police station in Whispering Falls when she saw you."

"Yes. Hi, Beth." I looked at the man.

"This is her boyfriend, Brent." Adeline pointed to the man.

"Brent," I whispered to myself and wanted to say, the daddy of Gabby's baby, but I kept that to myself.

There was a lot more going on here than selling Lifestyle products.

"Yes, ma'am." He looked down at me and extended his hand. "Can I help you up?"

I took his hand. There was an electrical shock that stunned me, knocking my intuition into high gear. Images of him and Gabby played like a movie in my head. There was a brief moment of them embracing that led straight into a fight with someone but not Beth. My mouth dried, I swallowed as the image of the black locust seed packet came to the forefront of my vision. I blinked a couple of times before the vision turned to the cashmere pink blanket that the teens lead me and Eloise to in the woods, ending with an image of Brent sobbing with his head buried in his hands. My palms began to sweat out his left over tears that triggered my vision.

"Are you sure you're okay?" He asked.

"I'm fine. I'm just a little thirsty." I smiled at him. He must've noticed me looking at his eyebrow.

"I'll grab a water." Adeline hurried off, leaving me standing there with Beth and Brent.

"That's a birthmark." He smiled. It was warm and gentle. My heart sank. I knew right then that he wasn't the killer and he was in love with Gabby, but he was Beth's boyfriend.

The pieces of this puzzle was becoming very clear and all I had to do was take all my evidence back to Oscar so he could get warrants to search Beth and her background to put her at the scene of the crime.

"Here you go." Adeline had an armful of bottled water and each one of us took one.

I watched as Beth declined and said she was going to set up before the other store managers got there. Brent took a couple of drinks before he tossed it into the public trashcan outside of the employee break room.

"I'll take that," I muttered to myself and grabbed a tissue out of my bag before I carefully took out his bottle of water. "I need your DNA."

Without telling Adeline that I was leaving, Mr. Prince Charming and I got back in the Green Machine and headed straight back to Whispering Falls, not stopping until we pulled in to Two Sisters and a Funeral.

Chapter Twenty-Three

"Why? Why can't you just check the DNA from this water bottle with the DNA of the baby?" I asked Constance Karima.

"Because you aren't the law." She waddled out of the autopsy room. The blue plastic apron was tied so tight around her girth, she looked like she was about to be cut in half. "Besides, when we were seeking confirmation on smelling death, you were quick to dismiss us." She tugged on the edges of the yellow rubber gloves that were pulled all the way up to the crock of her elbow.

"Dismissed us. Mmmhmmmm," Patience ho-hummed as she leaned over top of Gabby's body that was lying on the steel table with a big spot light hanging over her.

"Such a charming corpse." Constance smiled at the dead girl.

"That's an odd thing to say," I couldn't keep my mouth shut. "Especially since she was blackmailing Leah LeRoy."

"She was what?" Constance looked at me. Her eyes grew bigger from behind her magnified glasses. "Blackmailing?"

"Blackmailing?" Patience took an interest too.

"Did I say that?" I drew my hand up to my lips as if I let something slip, but in reality, I knew I had to entice them with something to get the information I needed to make sure my intuition was right. Not that I wasn't listening to my gift, but when you accuse someone of murder and get it wrong, it's a big deal.

"What is it you want again?" The little bit of gossip peaked Constance's interest.

"Oscar told me that Gabby was pregnant. I have reason to believe that her best friend, Beth Phipps, is the killer." I pulled out the bottle of water from my bag.

Constance walked a little closer. Patience put down the scrapple and hurried over to see what was in the bag.

"I believe that Beth's boyfriend is the father of the baby." I held the water bottle up in the air. "The boyfriend drank from this water bottle and I'd like to know if the baby shares the same DNA because if it does, then Leah LeRoy could be off the hook."

"Why aren't you letting Oscar do his job? Leah is a spiritualist." Constance wasn't budging.

"Leah is accused of killing a mortal. Which means that their laws are completely different and if we don't get this figured out, they will send in a prosecutor who will be here getting DNA and disrupting our little secret village." I wondered if I could tap into her emotional side of living here and how we have our special world, that she'd do it for me.

"Yes. The mortal police will be here, sister," Patience nodded. She reached out for the bottle.

"Don't touch it!" Constance instructed her. Patience quickly drew her hand back. "What is it about the blackmailing?"

"Gabby saw Leah doing some magic. Since then, Gabby has been blackmailing her to go public with it if Leah didn't agree to host a Lifestyle party here in Whispering Falls. She'd been trying to get in here for a long time." I looked between them. "Long story short, I traced back some yarn Leah had sold to a mortal man with a light brow. I found a baby blanket deep in the woods using the same yarn and," I rotated my wrist and hand in the air, "using my gift, I know this was a baby blanket made with that yarn sold to that man for this baby." I pointed to Gabby.

"How did you get the bottle?" Constance asked, she held her hand out in front of Patience, who was once again going after the bottle.

"Oscar asked me to look into some things and I took a job at Lifestyle so I could get in. Beth had tried to undercut Gabby at a few shops and when I was setting up for a party about an hour ago, Beth comes in with this light brow guy. My gift went nuts inside of me and that's when I knew it had to be him. He drank from the bottle and I took it." I jabbed the bottle out in front of me again for them to take it. "Listen, I know Leah LeRoy didn't kill Gabby Summerfied. This is our only hope if we are going to keep her out of mortal prison."

"Listen to June," Oscar said when he walked into the door. "I heard what you did."

"I know you're probably not happy that I went undercover, but I was going to tell you before you told me about Sonny." I held the bottle towards him. "This has the DNA on it. Plus now they have the blanket.

"If we can get his DNA to match the baby, then we can put the two together." He looked at Constance. "If we can prove Beth not only was jealous of how well Gabby was doing with the Lifestyle and had been trying to undercut

Gabby, then to find out her boyfriend cheated on her with Gabby and add to that a baby," Oscar's voice trailed off.

"Sister," Constance said to Patience and pointed to the bottle.

Patience reached up and gripped her hand around the bottle. There was a gleam her eyes that compared to a glassy volcanic rock. The corners of her mouth started to curl that grew into a thin-lipped smile before her mouth flew open, her head flew back, and scornful laugh came from the depths of her body.

"I don't know who killed me but I do know that I don't regret what Brent and I did. We are in love and he never loved Beth. When he told her about the baby, she went crazy and I don't care what she says, she's not my best friend." Patience's sweet and quiet voice had turned into an evil squeal.

She squeezed the bottle so tight, the top popped off and the water shot out in an arched stream, hitting Gabby's belly, disappearing inside of her.

"She's gone." Patience's head dropped as the bottle fell from her hand, hitting the ground next to her.

"What was is, sister?" Constance wrapped her arms around Patience. "What did you get?"

Oscar and I stood there in silence, not sure what had just happened.

"He is definitely the father. He didn't kill her." Patience's eyes drew up from the ground and she looked at Oscar. "Beth."

"Beth did it?" Constance questioned her.

"Beth did it. Mmmhhhmmmm. Beth did it," Patience repeated and began to act like her normal self.

We waited until Patience seemed to be completely back to normal from her ghost reading of Gabby, and to make sure they did a real DNA test on the bottle and the baby so that when Sonny did come from Locust Grove to Whispering Falls that we'd have all the mortal question T's crossed and I's dotted.

"This could get a little tricky," Oscar said when we got into the Green Machine to drive it back to the house. "I'm going to have to let Leah go but keep her on the suspect list. I think we've got plenty of evidence against Beth to bring her in on suspicion. Since that gives me a mortal and a spiritualist, maybe the Marys won't come."

"It's not the Marys I'm so worried about now. It's the Locust Grove sheriff department coming in here and putting a spotlight on our village." My concern and motivation for solving the case had definitely changed.

"When were you going to tell me about the teaching position?" he bowed his head and asked in a murmur.

"How did you find out?" I put the gearshift in park when we pulled up to the house. "Not that I wasn't going to tell you. I was going to wait until we solved Gabby's murder."

"Your Aunt Helena stopped by." He put his hand on the door, then swung around to look at me. "She was ever so happy to tell me about it."

"She shouldn't've done that. I'm sorry." I went to place my hand on his shoulder, but he jerked to get out of the car. "Are you mad?" I followed him into the house.

"No. I'm hurt. I love you and want you to follow your heart, but to find out from someone else, that hurts." He leaned against the kitchen counter with his arms crossed.

"When I was with those young witches today, it was so natural to me to show them the correct way to really use their intuition to create the perfect potion, not just any potion." I found myself smiling at the memory.

"You already took the job and taught a class?" He asked, with furrowed brows, throwing his hands up in the air.

"No. No." I shook my head. "It came out wrong. I went to Hidden Hall to get some cauldron cleaner." I bit my lip and realized I'd not checked on Leah. I looked past Oscar's shoulder, out the window, and down the hill, focusing my sights on A Charming Cure.

"While you were there, you decided to go to intuition school and teach without telling me?" He was more accusing me than asking me. He pushed himself up to stand and started to walk down the hall towards our bedroom.

"Oscar, aren't you going to let me explain?" I asked but my words met his hand, palm out.

"Stop." He shook his head. "I'm tired. I worked all night last night and I've got a big day ahead of me tomorrow." He turned back towards the bedroom. "I know you're going to the shop right now. I saw you looking out the window. Be sure to tell Leah that she's not the only suspect. That should make her feel better. You and I can talk in the morning."

He took a couple of more steps until he reached the bedroom. He shut the door behind him.

Chapter Twenty-Four

The look on Leah LeRoy's face when I went back to the shop and told her about what I'd uncovered about Beth Phipps, was priceless. I wished I could've been as happy as she was, but my little tiff with Oscar about the teaching position was what was taking up my time.

I wanted to let Oscar sleep, so I sent Leah home, closed the shop and restocked the shelves like I did every night.

Mr. Prince Charming was standing at the door when I looked up from rearranging a few bottles on a display table near the front of the shop.

"You. Where have you been?" I asked when I opened the door and juggled a couple of bottles in my hands.

The rush of a wind swept across my head, making me duck. I dropped the bottles and they scattered on the floor.

"What in the world?" I stood up, ignoring the mess as the owl hovered over me with its wings spread as wide as the shop.

Mr. Prince Charming did figure eights around my ankles. This helped ease any sort of anxiety or worry about the owl.

"You must be KJ's owl," I whispered. My heart stopped beating as rapidly and my breathing returned to normal. I'd never used this form of spying, so I had no idea how this played out.

The owl didn't bother looking at me. It was the wings where I found my answers. They were still and the feathers began to blend together in a white canvas just as the images of the past twenty-four hours of Beth Phipps life had begun to play like a movie.

It showed Beth leaving Whispering Falls, after I'd told her about the baby, in a hurry. There were a couple of times that she almost drove her car off the road. After she'd made it back into Locust Grove, she went to a house that I didn't recognize. It was more in the affluent area and since we were on the poor side, I never even ventured over to that side of the town.

The door of the house opened, and Brent walked out. Before Brent could get a word out, Beth smacked him right across the face. The two were arguing. Beth was pacing while Brent was swiping his hand through his hair and gesturing as if he were trying to explain. Beth looked fed up and got back in her car. She continued to drive erratically through the town until she got to the strip mall where Lifestyle was located. She was all smiles as she put her packages in the trunk of her car. She'd gone back to her house where she got ready for what appeared to be a Lifestyle party. She made a few phone calls after the party, one of which I bet was the sales numbers to Nina, the other I didn't know. But she went to bed. The next day it seemed like it was typical. She got up. Brent came over. She didn't look like she was forgiving him, but then they got into her car and parked at the Piggly Wiggly.

I was about to just tell the owl I'd seen enough when I noticed she and Brent hadn't gone back to her house. They'd gone to another house where they were tearing up the insides. Beth was rummaging through drawers and Brent was going through the closet. When I noticed Brent pick up some of Leah's crocheted bags, I knew they had to be at Gabby's house. When they left the house, the owl had focused in on the street address. The owl wings returned to normal as he hovered over me and Mr. Prince Charming.

I walked over to the door and opened it. The owl's wings drew in and he was sucked out into the dark night sky.

"What are we waiting for?" I looked over at Mr. Prince Charming. "We have go to Gabby's to see what they were looking for."

He darted out ahead of me. I locked the door behind me and we darted up the hill to the house. The lights were off and I knew Oscar had really gone to bed. There was no need to wake him up. He was tired, and I had no idea what I was going to find, if anything, so Mr. Prince Charming and I jumped into the Green Machine and sped out of town.

The normal thirty-minute drive was only about twenty since I'd found my heavy foot. Mr. Prince Charming had sat still in the passenger seat and stared out the window like he was a person.

"She must've been making good money." I bent my head down to see better outside of the windshield at the two-story home with the circular drive and waterfall in the front. "No wonder Beth was jealous of the income and clients."

I pulled the Green Machine down the street and parked. I'd not been real successful at breaking and entering, so I wanted to think that I was just there to help out a friend. Leah LeRoy.

Mr. Prince Charming went ahead of me. I put my back up against the shrub line to help blend in with the shadows of the fallen night. If I'd planned a little better, I should've brought some sort of spells with me, but when my intuition kicked in, it was hard to listen to common sense and be prepared.

I'd walked around to see if I could see if anyone was home, but all the lights were out and there weren't any cars pulled into the drive or the garage.

Mewl, mewl. Mr. Prince Charming alerted me to the back of the house. When I made it around there, he was standing underneath a cracked window. The problem was the window was much higher than I was tall. I turned around and looked to see what I could find that I could stand on so I could hoist myself up.

He ran deep into the dark night and I followed him to an old planter in the back near the brick out building. Next to the building was a full garden that Darla and Eloise would love to see. It was the lushest plantings I'd seen in a residential area. Gabby was really starting to impress me. I wonder why she'd resorted to blackmailing Leah.

"I guess this is what you want me to use." I sighed and dumped it over, dragging it underneath the window. "It sure does look like the perfect height." I stood back and looked at it after I'd flipped it over. "Here goes nothing."

I stepped up on the planter and lifted up the window before I hoisted myself up and over, falling into the laundry room.

It didn't look like she did any sort of laundry because there were so many dry-cleaning bags hanging on the bar. They were suits and pants that I didn't see Gabby wearing.

Meow. Mr. Prince Charming had jumped up on the window and balanced himself on the sill.

"What do you think Gabby had that Beth wanted?" I asked him before I turned to go into the house.

With a quick sweep of the first floor, there wasn't anything that stuck out to me. She lived a lavish life and I was a bit taken back. The furniture was first class and high dollar leather, marble, and tile. She'd spared no expense.

Mr. Prince Charming headed up the stairs and stopped to make sure I was following him. I tiptoed up the steps out of habit of sneaking around and went into the room where Mr. Prince Charming had disappeared.

I flipped on the light and realized I was in her office. As I walked around, I noticed she'd had some framed photos of Brent. The left-over yarn from the baby blanket was in the seat of one of the chairs. In the corner were a couple of boxes like the ones I'd seen at Lifestyle.

Rowl, rowl. Mr. Prince Charming screeched from the door.

"If you wanted my attention, you just got it." His yelp made my heart jump and go right back into the rapid beating.

He ran down the hall and I followed him to a bathroom. It had marble tiled flooring with one of those claw-footed tubs and stand up shower surrounded by glass walls. The double-sink counter was the exact same marble with very fancy gold knobs.

"What's this?" I looked down into the bowl and noticed there were a few empty bottles of Lifestyle in the sink. In the other sink, there were full bottles of Lifestyle. On the floor was a box like the ones I'd seen at the Lifestyle office.

I picked up one of the full bottles from the sink and noticed an oil line. I held it up to the light. There was a very distinct line between the oil and what appeared to be water.

My eyes darted from the box, to the empty bottles to the full bottles and back again until I finally got the nudge that told me I was now on the right track.

"Was Gabby making so much money because she was watering down the product?" I asked myself and laughed at how ridiculous that sounded. I looked down at the bottles. "Why would she be watering down the oils?"

I brought the bottle to my nose. Geranium, Fennel, Carrot Seed, Palmarosa, and Vitex swept along my nose hairs and deep into my soul.

"Baby." I took another sniff. "Was she worried about the baby or maternity leave?"

I gripped the bottle in my palm and squeezed, trying to get anything from my intuition about what was going on in Gabby's bathroom. I knew this had something to do with her death, but not sure what.

The bottle warmed, and I opened my palm. The ingredients were bubbling and swirling like I'd seen in Madame Torres's ball. Her words filtered into my memory.

"Look deep into the depths of the raging water to see. It'll be me you seek and be. The mix of smells will bring you closure, but not until a few days will be over," I repeated the words. "The inside is raging. I smell those baby ingredients and I know she was pregnant with Brent's baby and it's been a few days. What am I missing?"

Rowl! Mewl! Rowl!

I jumped around, dropping the bottle on the marble floor when I saw Mr. Prince Charming in net dangling down from the grips of Nina Teeter.

"I think you are missing this." Her nose curled over top of a disgusted look on her face.

"Nina, let him go." I took a step towards her.

"I don't think so. He broke into my house along with you." She dragged her other arm from around her body and pointed a gun at me.

"This is your house?" I asked somewhat confused since I thought it was Gabby's.

"Whose house did you think you were in?" She glared.

"Gabby's." I gulped.

"Gabby? Do you think she sold that much Lifestyle to live like this?" She cackled. "Hardly," she said with a sarcastic tone. "I wasn't sure what your sudden plan today was when you came into the office with a sudden change of heart and eagerness to start right then. So, who are you working for?"

"You. Lifestyle." I tried to take my eyes off the gun, but I couldn't. Out of the corner of my eye, I could see the Mr. Prince Charming was as cool as a cucumber while I was dying inside. "Please let my cat go."

"Why? Because you're going to have some sort of need for a therapy session?" She cackled. "You won't be alive long enough for that."

"I don't understand." I took a step back and tripped over the box. I grabbed the drawer from the sink and it fell out along with me on the marble floor, dumping out all its contents.

"Bravo." Nina took a step forward. "Now I just have to shoot you."

"No." I looked at a few of things that'd fallen out. There was an empty black locust seed packet just like the one that KJ had given me. "No. You killed Gabby?"

"Like you didn't know." She walked over and kicked the empty packet away from me. "Get up."

I did exactly what she said. I grimaced when she stuck the gun in my back.

"I want you to just walk softly, back down the steps and into the laundry room where you entered my house." She jutted the gun deeper, making me cringe. I moved slowly and it felt like hours as I walked down the hall and started down the steps.

"Why did you kill her? Wasn't she making good money for you?" I asked.

With each step, I recalled the owl's message.

"The baby. Brent is your son." My voice cracked.

"I really wanted a grandchild, but when Gabby refused to do what the boss said and wanted to turn me into the police because she said I was selling a deceptive product, then I knew that she'd be a horrible mother. Why would I do that to an innocent baby?" She retorted angrily.

"But you have a wonderful product." If I had to kiss her feet to get out of this situation, I was going to. "And I don't know what you did to her, but I can keep a secret. Just let me and my cat go."

I flung forward as she gave me a shove into the laundry room. She dropped the net and Mr. Prince Charming came scurrying out and over to me. She pointed her gun straight at me and pulled her cell phone out of her pocket.

"Who are you calling?" I asked.

"Yes. Police," she gasped like she was out of air. "Come quick. I had a robber and I. . . I . . . " she sounded pitiful, "I shot them and I think they're dead."

She dropped the phone.

"No," I begged.

Her sick sense of humor took over and she laughed in my face as her answer.

"I will get off free and clear if I've shot an intruder. And I'm taking the fact I killed Gabby to save not only the life of my company, but the future of my son, Brent and his future. He gave into Gabby when he had a wonderful thing going with Beth." She see-sawed the gun back and forth before she brought it up to my head. "Beth isn't the best salesperson, but with Gabby's clients and her knowing and being just fine with it, we can sell the watered-down oils with no problem." She laughed menacingly. "I mean, the clients have no idea and after all, it's the smell that sells them."

"How did you know about the black locust?" I gulped trying to buy some more time. If the cops were coming I could at least try and scream when they got here.

"Did you see my garden out there?" She asked with flat and unreadable stone eyes. "Black locust seeds are so hard to get ahold of. I went back to Locust Grove and told my son that I wanted him to go and pick out a yarn for the baby because I couldn't wait to make it a baby blanket, which was all a lie." She smiled. "He was so happy that I was starting to embrace the news that was secret. Really, I just wanted him to distract the young woman that Gabby had been praising. I knew they'd had a fight. I knew Gabby was getting the run around by Leah, so it was a perfect set up. I encouraged Gabby to keep pestering her to get her product into Whispering Falls and book a party because it would go along with my plan."

"You mean you planned to kill Gabby on the night she was in Whispering Falls because it was a perfect set up for Leah to look like the killer?" I asked as all the clues started to form the full puzzle.

There was a rattling sound coming from the door.

"That must be the police. Time's up." She pointed the gun and took a step forward placing the gun on my forehead.

Rowl! Mr. Prince Charming leapt up in the air and stuck his claws in her eyes, knocking her backwards just as the gunshot rang in the air, hitting the window behind me.

"Police! Put down the weapon!" The loud officer's voice was music to my ears.

"In here!" I yelled over and over until the blue dressed officer was standing at the laundry room door with his gun pointed on Nina.

Chapter Twenty-Five

"You scared me last night." Oscar recalled the events of previous evening.

"If she hadn't called the police thinking that she was going to kill me first, I probably would be dead." I'd gotten home late after giving the Locust Grove police my statement and after they'd collected evidence.

"I called Faith Mortimer to ask her to work in your shop today, because you need the day off." He filled my mug up with coffee. "I took the day off and left a note on the door of the station with my cell phone to call me if there was a problem."

"Only in Whispering Falls." I laughed and took a drink. "You wouldn't have believed Mr. Prince Charming. He was so awesome. He stabbed her in the eyes."

Mr. Prince Charming lifted his head from the top of the couch, yawned and laid it back down like it was no big deal.

"I do owe him." Oscar looked over at the lounging cat, giving me a little hope that the two of them would become friends after all. "First, I think we should go for a walk."

"A walk?" I was intrigued.

"It's a beautiful morning and I'm beyond blessed you are okay. Not only that, but I got news that the Order of Elders had detoured back to wherever they were because they'd heard about Leah LeRoy being freed. And," he hesitated, "you singlehandedly kept Locust Grove police from coming here and snooping around."

I got up and put my shoes on. It was already almost lunch time. I'd slept in and was taking it easy. The summer season was going to be starting next week and it was going to be a busy one. I could feel it in my gut.

"Leah was thrilled to open her shop today." Oscar was in the cupboards putting together a picnic lunch. "She said that she wanted to stop by later and see you. Which, I think a lot of people want to see you, so we better get going while we have time."

We decided to walk towards the wheat field and away from Whispering Falls. The birds sang along side of us while we walked. The sunshine was beating down on our faces and we got got absorbed in talking about the life we'd made for ourselves. It was a long way from where we started out underneath the tree eating Ding Dongs in his front yard.

"Speaking of Ding Dongs." He stopped, and I stopped. He pulled a couple of Ding Dongs from the bag. "This looks like a perfect spot to stop for a treat."

I looked up to see where we'd ventured off to.

"Oscar?" I questioned when I realized we were stopped at a tree right in front of the Intuitions School at Hidden Hall~A Spiritualist University.

"I figured we better get used to this view if you're going to take the teaching position here in the fall." His smile made my heart melt.

"You mean that you want me to take the job?" I asked and searched his face for some answers. "What about us? How can we be apart a few nights?"

"I talked to Colton. He said that he'd cover anytime that I needed off. If you want to stay here a few days with you or you want to come home, we can make it work. But you won't know if you love teaching unless you try it." He held the delicious treat up to my mouth and fed me a bite. "Wherever you go, June Heal, is where I go."

Mewl, mewl! Mr. Prince Charming came from behind the tree.

"And wherever I go, he goes." I held one arm out for Oscar and one arm out for Mr. Prince Charming, bringing them both closer to me.

It was strange how things happened. Not just in the spiritual world but how both worlds collided. If it weren't for Gabby, and how she made me realize life was so short and that I should take all the opportunities that came my way, then I'm not sure I'd have taken the job.

But with Oscar and Mr. Prince Charming's support, I knew that I, June Heal, had a great deal more to accomplish in the world. Mortal or otherwise.

About the Author

Tonya has written over 40 novels and 4 novellas, all of which have graced numerous bestseller lists including USA Today. Best known for stories charged with emotion and humor, and filled with flawed characters, her novels have garnered reader praise and glowing critical reviews. She lives with her husband, two very spoiled schnauzers and grew up in the small southern Kentucky town of Nicholasville. Now that her four boys are grown boys, Tonya writes fulltime.

Visit Tonya:
Facebook at Author Tonya Kappes,
https://www.facebook.com/authortonyakappes

Kappes Krew Street Team
https://www.facebook.com/groups/208579765929709/

Webpage
tonyakappes.com

Goodreads
https://www.goodreads.com/author/show/4423580.Tonya_Kappes

Twitter
https://twitter.com/tonyakappes11

Pinterest
https://www.pinterest.com/tonyakappes/

For weekly updates and contests, sign up for Tonya's newsletter Kappes Krew Weekly via her website or Facebook.

Also by Tonya Kappes

Magical Cures Mystery Series
A CHARMING CRIME
A CHARMING CURE
A CHARMING POTION (novella)
A CHARMING WISH
A CHARMING SPELL
A CHARMING MAGIC
A CHARMING SECRET
A CHARMING CHRISTMAS (novella)
A CHARMING FATALITY
A CHARMING DEATH (novella)
A CHARMING GHOST
A CHARMING HEX
A CHARMING VODOO
A CHARMING CORPSE

Killer Coffee Mystery Series
SCENE OF THE GRIND
MOCHA AND MURDER
FRESHLY GROUND MURDER
COLD BLOODED BREW

Spies and Spells Mystery Series
SPIES AND SPELLS
BETTING OFF DEAD
GET WITCH or DIE TRYING

A Laurel London Mystery Series

CHECKERED CRIME
CHECKERED PAST
CHECKERED THIEF

A Divorced Diva Beading Mystery Series
A BEAD OF DOUBT SHORT STORY
STRUNG OUT TO DIE
CRIMPED TO DEATH

Olivia Davis Paranormal Mystery Series
SPLITSVILLE.COM
COLOR ME LOVE (novella)
COLOR ME A CRIME

Grandberry Falls Series
THE LADYBUG JINX
HAPPY NEW LIFE
A SUPERSTITIOUS CHRISTMAS (novella)
NEVER TELL YOUR DREAMS

Bluegrass Romance Series
GROOMING MR. RIGHT
TAMING MR. RIGHT

Women's Fiction
CARPE BREAD 'EM

Young Adult
TAG YOU'RE IT

A Ghostly Southern Mystery Series
A GHOSTLY UNDERTAKING

A GHOSTLY GRAVE
A GHOSTLY DEMISE
A GHOSTLY MURDER
A GHOSTLY REUNION
A GHOSTLY MORTALITY
A GHOSTLY SECRET

Kenni Lowry Mystery Series
FIXIN' TO DIE
SOUTHERN FRIED
AX TO GRIND
SIX FEET UNDER
DEAD AS A DOORNAIL

Southern Cake Baker Series
Written by Tonya Kappes
Pen Name: Maymee Bell
CAKE AND PUNISHMENT
BATTER OFF DEAD

Copyright

Made in the USA
Lexington, KY
24 April 2018